ROGUE WARRIOR

SUSAN GAYLE

ZEBRA BOOKS
KENSINGTON PUBLISHING CORP.

ZEBRA BOOKS are published by

Kensington Publishing Corp.
850 Third Avenue
New York, NY 10022

First Zebra Printing: June, 1996
10 9 8 7 6 5 4 3 2 1

Printed in the United States of America

To Terra Ashley who will be surprised to find out that I admire her very much. Her willingness to strive for her goals against great odds has inspired me. Her search for the balance between work, children and her own life reminds me about what is truly important. Her success allows me to picture my own victories. May life bring you all things good, dear friend.

And

A special "thank you" to Lt. Stuart Broce for information on the technical world and emotional lives of fighter pilots in general, and F-14 pilots in particular. He was most forthcoming with his assistance. The needs of fiction required some bending of the truth, for which I accept responsibility.

One

The F-14 jet moved swiftly through the twilight like a phantom predator soaring on currents of air. On all sides, the darkening sky stretched forever, blurring slightly on the edges of the horizon. Thousands of feet below waves swelled and crashed against the sides of the carrier, but up here there was only the night, the men and the machine.

Michael Coburn adjusted his mask and stared to his right, watching the stars rise. Cassiopeia, a fall constellation, remained stubbornly out of view. She was his favorite. There wasn't any reason. No one had told him a significant story about that particular cluster. As a boy he'd seen the heavens as something to be conquered, not admired.

"But she sure is pretty," he said softly.

"You say something, sir?" his Radar Intercept Officer asked from the rear of the cockpit.

Mike cursed under his breath. It wasn't like him to be caught daydreaming. "Not a thing, Winston. What's on the screen?"

"Nothing, sir."

The formality made him smile. It was his Radar Intercept Officer or RIO's first assignment on a carrier. He'd had only a couple of weeks back in Miramar before the squadron had shipped out. Winston was as green as spring grass and about as sophisticated. He came from some tiny town in Kansas. Mike fingered the control stick. It would be easy enough to send the jet into a dive straight for hell. The kid might lose more than his lunch, but it would take care of the "sir" crap.

The crackling over his headset alerted Mike to a message from the carrier.

"Rogue 112, this is Gray Ghost," the disembodied voice intoned. "Your signal return to base. How copy?"

"Rogue 112, roger," Mike answered. "How about that, Winston? They're calling us home." He glanced at his watch. "If we're lucky, they'll still be serving dinner in the mess."

"Yes, sir. I'd like that, sir."

Mike sighed. It was going to be a long tour. Before beginning the turn back to the carrier, he glanced toward the eastern horizon. Two stars twinkled back at him. Cassiopeia was rising. He saluted her, then eased the large jet into a sweeping curve that headed west.

The tail hook went down with a satisfying *thunk*.

"Know what that is, Winston?"

"Yes, sir!" Mike could hear the fear in the boy's voice.

"You ever land on a carrier before?"

"No, sir."

"You ever throw up on a plane?"

The boy coughed. "Not since I was a kid, sir."

Mike grinned. Yeah, a kid. What did that make him? Winston was maybe twenty. It was enough to make a thirty-four-year-old man feel ancient.

The clear black night allowed him to see for eight or ten miles, but below the jet there was only darkness. He knew the carrier sat out on the ocean, bobbing like a sick duck, but he wouldn't see it until it was too late to change his mind. The radar beeped softly, showing their approach. Controls glowed.

He lowered the landing gear and instantly felt the slight drag on the plane. He dropped the flaps next, then scanned the water. There.

"You see her, Winston?"

"Yes, sir. She sure looks tiny from up here."

"You got that right, kid."

The headset crackled again. "Rogue 112, you're at three-quarters of a mile. Call the ball."

The ball, the control of the landing, passed from carrier to pilot. "112, Tomcat ball." He glanced at his fuel gauge. "4.2." That told the carrier how much fuel he had left and if he could afford to make a second pass before landing.

Even though he was seconds away from touching down, time slowed to a crawl. The carrier moved almost due west, but the runway stood at a ten degree angle. The lights grew brighter as he approached. For those last two heartbeats, he stopped breathing. Everything disappeared except for the controls and the narrow, short, bobbing runway.

Now!

The wheels hit a split second before the arresting cable jerked the plane to a bone-jarring halt.

But something was wrong. His hand! It couldn't work the control stick! His fingers didn't bend, didn't respond. He tried to keep the jet level, tried to keep them on the runway. He reached across his body to grab the controls with his still-functioning left hand. He was too late.

He stared in disbelief as the jet careened off the carrier. He waited for the crash when they hit the water, but there was nothing but dead silence and black pain. His heart pounded, and he realized the silence had been broken by screams of torment. It was only then that he knew the screams were his own. His hand. His hand. My God, why?

The question woke him, as it had every morning since the accident.

He'd heard of injured men who had a few moments reprieve each day. Those foggy half-seconds, when they were allowed to forget the pain and the loss. He had no such blessing. It was his first thought every morning. Why?

Mike kept his eyes closed. It was just a dream, he told himself. None of it was real. Except for his hand.

Still keeping his eyes shut, he forced his right hand to close into a fist. Pain shot up his arm. He clenched his teeth and strained until the tips of his fingers touched his palm. Sweat popped out on his face and chest. Cursing fate and life and anyone who would listen, he exhaled and let his fingers return to their relaxed position.

Loss of fine motor skills, the doctor had said. Seventy percent recovery possible. With work. Mike fought back a groan. It had been six months and he'd barely recovered forty percent. Hell, what did it matter? Even if the doctor was right, seventy percent wasn't good enough to fly jets.

Mike slowly opened his eyes and stared at the ceiling. It was almost dawn. There was nothing to get up for, but if he didn't, Grady would be pounding on his door and demanding to know what was wrong. The old man didn't know Mike still had the dream. He didn't need to know.

Mike sat up, then reached for the jeans crumpled by the side of the bed. He pulled them on and rose. The partial numbness made his fingers feel swollen and uncontrollable. He'd mastered simple tasks like picking up blocks and holding a glass, but anything that needed delicate control—like buttons—required intense effort. The button fly took almost five minutes to fasten. By the time he was done, sweat coated his chest and back and he was shaking with frustration.

At the hospital, the nurse had tried to get him to wear zip-up jeans with a velcro closure. He'd told her exactly what she could do with those jeans. He'd worn button-flies his whole life, and nothing was going to change that fact.

He stared at his right hand. In the half-light, the ugly scars blurred until they were barely visible. The doctor had told him that with time he'd develop the use of his left hand. It wasn't impossible to relearn to write and master other skills. There was every reason to believe he would live a normal life.

Right, Mike thought grimly. The man had more degrees than common sense. Even the Navy had known enough to cut the wounded officer loose.

After pulling on socks and boots, he slipped on a shirt, but left it open. The buttons could wait. He walked down the long hallway to the stairs, then into the kitchen. The sky lightened with each passing minute. After plugging in the coffee pot, he opened the refrigerator and stared at the meager contents. One egg. Three six-packs. Some lettuce that looked ready to breed. He shook his head. He and Grady sure made a hell of a pair. The old man was trying to starve him into going to town, but Mike wasn't afraid of dying. He glanced at his hand, then slammed the refrigerator door shut.

From outside, the sounds of the morning had begun. Birds called to each other. Spring had come to the central California mountains. He stepped outdoors and inhaled the fresh, moist air.

To his left stood a large three-story building. He ignored it, much as he tried to ignore why it was there. But he couldn't ignore the smells. Fresh churned earth competed with cut wood and paint. The scent of the horses drifted to him, along with a lazy whinny. Hooves stomped against stalls. Without the sun to warm the air, the temperature remained in the forties. Mike shivered, but didn't bother to do up his shirt. It would take too damn long.

The construction trailers lined the area between the corrals and the new building. A mini-van sat in front of the barn. He frowned, trying to remember if it had been there last night. For the most part the workers stayed away from the horses. It amused him that burly contractors feared the large but gentle animals.

Walking away from the new building, he approached the stables. Trees heavy with spring foliage lined one side of the path. His land was too far south to support the majestic redwoods, but oak and pine, along with dozens of fruit trees, decorated his acreage. He stopped and looked back at the old house. The building needed paint and the porch sagged. Inside the plumbing was older than God. There was a time when he'd come to this valley and fallen in love with the land. The challenges had excited him. He and Grady had shared a dream for the ranch, had planned a future. Two old seadogs, settling down together. When Grady had retired two years ago, it had seemed so right. So perfect.

Mike looked away, unable to bear viewing the past and what should have been. It was ruined. Stolen by some quirk of fate, and the actions of a stupid kid who should be taken out and shot. No, he thought, again moving toward the barn. Shooting was too good for Tim Evans. What was supposed to have been a refuge for the future had become a penalty box in the present. And Mike's sentence was for life.

At the corral, a black gelding trotted up to greet him.

"Hey, boy," he murmured, awkwardly patting the animal's face with his good hand. "I didn't bring any sugar. I doubt there's any left. That stubborn old man won't go to town."

The gelding snuffled his hand, then snorted in disgust.

"Tell me about it," Mike said.

He stiffened. Carried on the slight breeze came a sweetly spicy aroma. Not completely floral, not musky, but definitely feminine. He inhaled sharply. He hadn't seen any women construction workers. It must be his imagination. Or it had been too long since he'd—

Mike shook his head. He had enough trouble without thinking about sex. Turning away from the corral, he leaned against the railing and stared up at the sky. The light from the rising sun washed away most of the stars, leaving behind a creamy paleness that would soon darken to blue.

"All the best ones are gone."

He spun when he heard the voice. Something moved in the shadows of the barn, then a woman stepped out into view. The darkness hid her features. He received a quick impression of medium height, casual clothes and shoulder-length dark hair.

"The stars, I mean," she said, moving closer to him. "The good ones have already set. I watched them." She joined him against the railing, her head dropping back as she stared straight up.

The scent of her perfume enveloped him, teasing, clawing at the doors he'd shut and locked. Six months at sea out of every eighteen for the last twelve years had taught him to appreciate the uniqueness of a woman's fragrance. Countless nights of pleasure had taught him to appreciate the potential of her body. The latter was lost to him now, but the former . . . He drew in another breath, deeper this time as if he could swallow the subtleties of the perfume and they would nourish him through the bleakness of the day.

"What do you know about stars?" he asked, ignoring the need to move closer.

"Nothing technical if that's what you're asking. I know I like them. They seem so bright and hopeful."

"By the time the light reaches here, most of them have burnt out."

"Golly, you're cheerful in the morning, aren't you? I suppose the Spanish Inquisition is a favorite time in history for you?"

He felt her looking at him. The negative comment had slipped out without thought. He'd wanted to call it back as soon as he'd said it. Getting lost in self-pity had never been the plan. He'd only wanted to stay lost. Hide. It had sounded so simple but the world kept intruding. First Grady, then the construction workers, and now her.

"So how do *you* know so much about the stars?" she asked. Her voice was low for a woman, but not unpleasantly so. Soft. At one time, it might have been appealing.

Tenacious, he thought, and wondered if he had enough decency left to apologize for being a jerk. The answer came quickly. No.

"I—" He paused. There was a time he would have grinned and said, "I fly among them, baby. Wish I could take you with me, but it's all top secret. I could show you, but then I'd have to kill you."

The dumb ones had sighed, obviously impressed with his importance and snuggled closer. The smart ones had rolled their eyes and forced him to work a little harder. He'd liked that best. But in the end, smart or dumb, he had them all. Everyone wanted to, just for a moment, or a quick lay, be one with a jet jockey. Anonymous pleasure for him, bragging rights for her.

He cleared his throat. Would "go away" be too subtle? "A former hobby."

"Really?" She sounded vaguely interested. "How do you handle the crick in your neck?"

Involuntarily, he glanced down at her and watched her rotate her head from side to side. "Occupational hazard."

She looked up at him. The sun still clung below the horizon as if too lazy to begin the day, but enough light stole across the sky to allow him to see her more clearly. Dark hair, thick and straight, hung down to her shoulders. Strong features, big brown eyes and a wide full mouth, dominated her face. A denim jacket painted with vivid colors hid most of her body from view. The unbuttoned front hung open, exposing jeans and a sweater. She came a little past his shoulder. Probably five-five or six to his six-two. Average, he thought, dismissing her. Except for that damn perfume.

The silence between them lengthened. She continued to study him. He caught her silent perusal out of the corner of his eye and tucked his right hand into his pocket.

Birds chirped. In one of the trailers, he heard a worker bang a coffee pot on a stove. The horses stirred in the barn and nickered to each other.

"This place is going to be terrific," she said at last.

He grunted.

"You've got a perfect location. The elevation of the valley is high enough to keep it from getting too hot in the summer. Isn't there a stream near by? Are there fish?"

She wasn't going away, he thought, then straightened up and faced her. "Who are you?"

"The decorator. I'm the design part of Ross Building and De-sign." She waved her arm to encompass the large building under construction. "You know, I pick out the wallpaper and carpets, the furniture. Supervise the finishing work."

"Great." Why the hell had he thought a dude ranch was a good idea?

"I'm not supposed to arrive until today," she said brightly. "I mean it *is* today, but I'm not supposed to arrive until later. I'm early."

He stared down at her. Sunlight drifted across them and picked up the gleam in her thick hair. She tossed it back with a careless gesture and smiled. Easy, confident. Alive. He pulled his hand out of his pocket and folded his arms across his chest.

"I couldn't sleep," she said shrugging her shoulders.

"What?"

"Last night." Her mouth pulled into a straight line. It was, he supposed, the closest she came to a frown. "I was all packed and ready to go, but I couldn't sleep, so I drove down from San Francisco. I like driving at night. It's just me and truckers. And I have the ghosts to keep me comfortable."

He knew he was getting older, but he hadn't expected his hearing to be the first thing to go. "Ghosts?"

"Oh! Sorry." She grinned. "I mean the past. You know, memories. Not real ghosts."

"Yeah, I know." He had plenty of those to keep him company, but unlike the ones belonging to the woman in front of him, they offered little companionship and no comfort.

"I wanted to beat the sunrise," she said.

"In God's name, why?"

"A new day." She hugged the open edges of the jacket to her body and drew in an exaggerated deep breath. "Can't you smell it? Spring, the promise of growth. Baby birds being born, plants sprouting. That's why I took this job. I love the country."

All he could smell was her and it was driving him crazy. Not with desire; he wasn't a complete fool. No, it was more those damn ghosts she'd mentioned. They haunted him with reminders of what had been before.

The woman leaned back against the railing. Behind her, in the corral, the gelding silently approached. Mike thought about warning her, but then decided it wasn't his business. Besides, he couldn't summon the energy. The horse slowed, then took one long step and stretched forward to smell her hair. His fat lips brushed the crown of her head.

Instantly she jumped forward and shrieked. The gelding bolted for the far side of the corral.

"It's just a horse," Mike said mildly, surprised to realize his lips were twitching.

She stared at the retreating animal and touched the top of her head. "I thought it was a bug. Yuck! I hate bugs." She shuddered. "You could have told me he was coming."

"I thought you liked nature. Baby birds and all that."

"Okay, so maybe I should have been more selective in my statement. I like all nature that doesn't have more than four legs."

"What about snakes?"

"Snakes?" She looked confused.

"Snakes don't have legs at all. Do you like them?"

"No." Dark eyebrows drew together in concentration. She planted fists on her hips. "Okay, no six-legged creatures, no snakes."

Again she tossed her head. Again he watched as her hair flew over her shoulders. It swung with a shiny grace that caught the rays of the rising sun. Thick, he thought from the way it moved. And heavy. Hair a man could bury his hands in to hold her still for his kiss.

He glanced down at his arms folded over his chest. If that man had hands that worked.

"What about lizards?" he asked, more to force his mind away from the thoughts of hands than because he cared about baiting her. "Lizards have only four legs."

She laughed then. The sound caught him off-guard, like a wind sheer at fifteen thousand feet. His stomach lurched. He found himself watching the flash of her white teeth against the grin of her mobile mouth.

"I confess," she said and leaned back against the corral. "I have every normal female squeamishness possible. I hate slimy things, blood and guts, snakes, lizards and bugs. I tolerate worms because they help plants grow. Have I passed or failed the interview?" Her wide smile belied any concern about the answer.

"It's not up to me. You're part of the package to build the dude ranch."

"Lucky me."

She sounded like she meant it. Cheerful and optimistic. He couldn't stand much more.

She raised her arms until her elbows rested on the top rail. The coat fell open exposing a thick sweater and worn but well-fitting jeans. Involuntarily, he catalogued her body. To sum it up in one word: curves. Long and lean had always been his type by choice, but he'd occasionally been tempted by others. There was something to be said for a woman who filled out her clothes.

The new decorator wasn't heavy, but she'd never pass for a model. Well-shaped thighs flowed into rounded hips. The hem of her sweater teased the button of her jeans and accentuated a narrow waist. Full breasts jutted out against her boldly patterned wool top. His gaze drifted to her throat and olive-toned skin exposed there, then back to her breasts. A man could feast there for days, he thought, knowing that part of him had long since died. He didn't even bother to wait for heat to flare in his groin; it wouldn't. A man could fill his hands with the feminine weight of her breasts and tease—

Hands. He turned away and faced the sunrise. It always came back to hands. He dropped his arms to his sides and wondered when it was all going to end. The doctors swore it would get better. The head shrinkers had promised a bright future. They'd all lied.

"You're not the chatty type, are you?" the woman asked.

"No."

"Then you can't be Sean Grady."

Mike thought of his friend. Again his mouth twitched. "Obviously you two have never met."

"We've spoken on the phone. He seems very nice."

"Don't let him hear you call him that."

"He doesn't like to be thought of as nice?"

Mike shook his head and half turned toward her. "He was in the Navy for twenty years. Got busted back several times for drinking and fights, among other things. He used to scare the—" He glanced over at the woman. "—the crap out of the new recruits. Intimidating green pilots was his favorite."

"Gee, you're making me nervous."

"Don't be. Grady's a sucker for pretty eyes."

"Thank you."

Her response was his first clue that he'd complimented her. The old lines died hard, he thought in disgust, then realized that she did have pretty eyes. Wide and dark, like a fawn's.

"If you're not Sean Grady, then you must be the mysterious Mike

Coburn," she said, pushing off the corral railing and stepping close to him. "The partner who's not supposed to be here."

"You got that right, lady."

"Will it be a short visit?" she asked.

"No. I'm the newest permanent resident." Even he heard the bitterness in his voice.

Either she was deaf or she chose to ignore it, for she held out her hand and smiled. "Great. I'd love to discuss my ideas with you. I'm Jessie Layton, decorator extraordinaire."

"Modest, too," he said, then glanced at her outstretched hand. He reached his arm forward, then drew it back. "I can't shake hands with you."

She frowned. "Why?"

"An accident. I can't judge my strength anymore."

"Oh."

He tensed, waiting for the inevitable discussion. What happened? Can you still fly? Next would come the pity. That's when people got silent, but he saw it in their eyes. The shifting and uneasy glances. Even without words, their bodies spoke of their need to get away, in case the failure was contagious.

Jessie just looked at his face. "Bummer," she said finally. "Then I guess arm wrestling for a raise is out of the question."

Instantly her eyes grew wide with horror. She covered her mouth with her palm.

Mike didn't know whether to laugh or slug her. But between his bad hand and her being a woman, the latter wasn't an option. That left laughing. One corner of his mouth quirked up.

"I'm sorry," she said, reaching out to touch his arm. Her fingers brushed the sleeve of his shirt. "Oh, Lord, I didn't mean to say that. It's just this is a new job and I'm really excited. I didn't sleep. Oh, that was in such bad taste. I can't *believe* I blurted that out."

Color stained her smooth cheeks. She stood close enough for him to feel the heat of her embarrassment. He didn't know women blushed anymore.

"Can you forgive me?" she asked. "I guess this is where I tell you that when I get nervous I tend to put my foot in my mouth. Although I haven't done it this badly in a long time."

"That must make your work interesting."

"Sometimes." She shrugged. "Sometimes not. Occasionally my

big mouth gets me fired. Once I was working with this rich old lady in San Francisco. You know, one of those old houses built right after the 1906 earthquake and fire. She wanted the guest rooms remodeled and redecorated. She'd picked out this carpet sample to show me. It was my first big job. I thought I was going to throw up, I was so nervous."

"What happened?" he asked, surprised to find out he was almost interested.

"She had this little dog. You know, one of those yappy things you're always scared of stepping on? Anyway, I was terrified of her and of the dog and the job. So when she showed me the carpet sample, I just blurted out that not only was it ugly, it was the color of dog, ah, refuse." Her head dropped until her chin rested on her chest.

"She fired you."

"You bet. The head of Ross Building and Design called me into his office and read me the riot act."

"What happened?"

Jessie looked up and smiled. "He got someone else to help the rich old lady and put me to work decorating his penthouse."

"Any dogs there?"

"No. And no embarrassing moments." She stuffed her hands into her coat pockets. "The good news is that I usually only have one outburst per client."

"So you won't say anything else even remotely offensive?"

She bit her lower lip. "I'm really sorry if I hurt your feelings."

He didn't have feelings to hurt, but she didn't have to know that. For a moment, he regretted not giving in to the impulse to laugh. After all, her direct comments were better than what happened here at the ranch. He knew the construction workers stared when they thought he wasn't looking. He knew what they were thinking. Pity. Embarrassment. Survivors guilt and relief that it wasn't them.

Mike tried to clench his fists, but the pain in his right hand reminded him that he couldn't even do that. He waited for the anger and the frustration to overtake him. Instead, there was nothing. Nothing except the knowledge it would always be like this.

He glanced at Jessie. "Don't sweat it," he said.

"Great. Let's shake on—" She thrust her arm out. "Oh, dear. I'm sorry. I need coffee."

"Lady, I think you need more help than that," he growled, knowing he was enjoying pretending to be angry at her just to get a reaction.

"Two is my absolute limit," she said earnestly. "I swear. Two gaffes and I'm done for a year."

He narrowed his eyes. "Right. How long have you had this foot-in-mouth disease?"

She swallowed. "All my life."

"That's about how my luck's been running these days."

"You know, Mr. Coburn, it's really early. I should probably go get something to eat. A little food, coffee, I'll be a new woman and we can start over. Is there a place to eat around here?"

"You remember that small town you passed about twenty miles before the ranch?"

She nodded.

"That's it."

"Oh. Well, I guess I'd better get going then. I'll be back in a couple of hours. The foreman should be up by then and—"

He jerked his head toward the old house. "There's an egg in the refrigerator. You and Grady can fight over it."

"One egg? Are you kidding?"

"I never kid."

Two

Jessie stared after Mike Coburn, but he didn't show any signs of waiting for her. She took that as an invitation to follow. A man of few words, she thought as she walked after him. Few words, little or no humor, although he'd been gracious about her arm wrestling slip.

Why? she asked herself, then shook her head, knowing there was no answer. It had happened all her life. As soon as she got nervous, her brain went into over-drive and her good sense went on vacation. She could still remember the horrified look on her mother's face the day she'd stopped a good-looking man on the street and asked him to have sex with her mother. She'd been looking for a baby sister, not soliciting. It wasn't her fault that she'd only recently been told the facts of life and had finally figured out why asking Santa Claus for a sibling wasn't getting any results.

It had all worked out, she reminded herself as she smiled. John and her mother had ended up dating for almost a year. Although they had never married, or produced the much-wanted baby sister, her mother had later confessed that John had very willingly complied with Jessie's initial request.

Mike reached the porch of the two-story house. He turned and stared out at the corrals. Pain tightened the lines of his face. Not physical pain, but a soul aching kind of hurt.

It was fully morning now, and she could view him clearly. Her first thought upon seeing him had been that he was much too handsome for his own good. She still thought that. He was the kind of man you'd follow home from the grocery store and not care that your ice cream was melting.

Blond and blue-eyed. Mid-thirties. Tall and muscled. And dangerous. Good-looking men were usually bad news for women. Everything came too easily for them. They didn't know about real life. She liked to think she was immune to the physical appeal. Her hormones told her otherwise.

Most of his hair had been brushed back from his face, but a few strands fell over his forehead. His tan accentuated the blue of his eyes. Despite the chill of the early morning, his cotton work shirt hung open, exposing the center of his hair-covered chest and the ripples of the muscles in his flat stomach. Jeans stretched on forever down to worn cowboy boots. All the surface trappings of a successful rancher were in place. But he didn't fit in.

Sean Grady had told her his partner wouldn't be part of the dude ranch for several years. What had happened to change that? Was it the accident that had injured his hand?

Mike continued to stare out at the horizon. She turned to see what he was looking at, but only saw the horses and the barn, a few trees and a blue sky that stretched on forever.

"My idea of heaven," she said softly.

"Hell," came the muttered response.

She spun to face him, but he continued to look beyond her. "This is too beautiful to be hell."

"How about prison?" He lowered his gaze suddenly and focused on her as if he'd just realized she was there. The pain in his eyes was quickly shuttered, but the bitter twist of his mouth remained.

What had he lost? Something horrible? It had to be, to hurt that much. A lover? A wife?

Jessie flipped her hair over her shoulder. That would explain many things. She knew about losing someone you cared about. It had been eighteen months, but she still had trouble believing Brandon was gone. Even when she'd told the story about the old lady firing her, it had been difficult not to cry. That had been the first time they'd met. She could still remember how he'd struggled to keep from laughing when she'd told him what had happened. By the time she'd finished decorating his penthouse, they'd' been engaged. Marriage had quickly followed.

Let it go, she told herself. But it wasn't that easy. Mike continued to stare down at her. She stepped onto the porch, but even there she had to look up to meet his gaze. He was a head taller.

"As prisons go, it's not so bad," she said finally.

"How would you know?"

"I wouldn't."

He looked faintly surprised, as if he'd expected some long-winded explanation about handling whatever crisis he found himself in. She barely knew the man; what did he expect her to say?

She scuffed her boot against the warped wooden floor of the porch. There were only about two feet separating her from Mike Coburn. She could feel the irritation—no, that wasn't strong enough—the rage circling through and around his body. His chest rose and fell in agitation. She stared at his bare skin. Why hadn't he buttoned his shirt? Her gaze dropped to his right hand, hanging at his side. Scars criss-crossed his fingers.

Maybe he couldn't.

That thought made her doubly wish she'd kept her mouth shut.

"Look's like it's going to be a warm one," she said, then wondered if she could apply for an award for the most inane remark spoken under pressure.

"I see you two have met."

Mike spun toward the front of the house. Jessie stepped to the side and saw a man standing in the doorway. Close to fifty, with bright red hair, he stood about an inch shorter than her. His blue eyes twinkled with amusement.

"It's a little early to be working," he said, walking toward her. His rolling gait spoke of his years at sea. The man stopped in front of her and held out his hand. "But I like a go-getter. Sean Grady, at your service. You must be Jessie."

She smiled and allowed his palm to engulf hers. "Yes. We meet at last."

Grady winked roguishly. "You're as pretty as your voice, but I imagine I'm a disappointment. You probably thought I'd be as tall and handsome as that boy over there." He squinted at Mike. "Don't think I'd like all that height; it'd make me dizzy. But I wouldn't mind being young again."

"You're not so old," she said.

Grady released her hand and grinned. "And he's not so young."

"In your dreams, old man," Mike said, then frowned as if he regretted joining the conversation.

"Ignore him," Grady said. "The coffee's ready, if you'd like some."

"Sounds wonderful. I drove down last night, and I'm about dead on my feet."

"Then what are we standing out here for? Coburn, you've got the manners of a mud-soaked sea snail." Grady held the screen door open for her.

As she walked past him, she glanced down at his forearm where his flannel sleeve had been rolled up to the elbow and saw an intricate tattoo of an eagle. The talons clutched a branch that ended just above his wrist bone. The bird's wings rested at its side, but each feather had been carefully drawn in exquisite detail.

"Wow. Did that hurt?"

Grady followed her gaze, then he squared his shoulders proudly. "Ain't she a beaut? Had it done in the Philippines. Back in sixty-eight. My first tour. Could get real work done then, by artists. Hurt? I was in the Navy, little lady. Navy men don't feel pain."

"Really? I thought that was the Marines."

He gave her a mock glare. She laughed and stepped into the house.

"I've got a tattoo of another bird on my back," he said, as he ushered her down the center of the building.

She had a brief impression of large rooms on either side, filled with worn but functional furniture. Past the living area was a dining room, then a door on the left opened to a big kitchen with a center island butcher block; a table and four chairs sat next to the bay window. Cupboards, a sink and refrigerator lined the wall opposite one window. A big stove with six burners stood against the other. She followed Grady inside.

"There's an American flag on this shoulder," he said, pointing, as he stopped beside the stove. "And a couple more I can't show you."

She folded her arms over her chest. "Oh?"

The old man grinned again. "Yet."

He reminded her of a bantam rooster showing off for his hens. Lines fanned out from the corners of his eyes. They deepened when he smiled, as if he often found pleasure in life. His ruddy complexion told of his years in the elements.

She leaned against the center island. "Your family is Irish?"

"With a name like Sean Grady, you have to ask?"

She hadn't heard Mike follow them, but now he stood behind her in the doorway.

"That's me," Grady said, ignoring Mike and answering her question. "Me dear departed mother, God rest her soul, brought us bairns over during the great potato famine." He sighed theatrically, an exaggerated brogue thickening his words. "Worked herself to an early death putting a few scraps of bread on our plates."

Behind her, Mike snorted.

Jessie was about to express her sympathy when vaguely remembered bits of history drifted through her mind. "Wait a minute. You aren't old enough to be a child of the famine. It was years before the first world war."

The old man didn't look the least bit concerned at being caught in the lie. "Maybe," he conceded. "But it makes a great story. Used to get the ladies all in a flutter to hear more."

"It's the nineties, Grady," she said, straightening. "You might want to try a more contemporary approach with women."

He picked up the coffee pot from the stove and poured the dark liquid into the mugs on the counter. "Could be. But why change something that's worked so well?"

"What does your wife say?"

"Yeah, Grady." Mike chuckled. "What *does* your wife say?"

Grady ignored him and handed her a full mug. "Do you take milk or sugar?"

"Yes, both, thanks." She didn't dare look behind to see Mike's expression.

"There isn't any," Mike said. "Milk, sugar, or a wife."

Grady pulled open the refrigerator. Jessie saw some beer, the lone egg that Mike had promised and a large slimy green thing that looked ready to start walking.

"What on earth is that?" she asked.

"Lettuce," Grady said. "There doesn't seem to be any milk."

"Or sugar," Mike said.

Grady walked to the cupboard and pulled it open. Jessie stared. Nothing. Not one scrap of food. A jar of pickles stood on the bottom shelf, but it was empty except for the liquid.

"Black is fine," she said, not wanting to distress her host. Hosts, she amended, thinking of Mike, but still refusing to look at him. She could feel him behind her. Breathing. She wanted to turn and see if he was still attractive. Obviously she'd been alone too long. He wasn't charming or the least bit friendly. So he shouldn't affect her at all.

"Are you sure?" Grady asked.

"It's great." She took a sip and almost gagged. Mocha mud. It would make a terrific facial.

"We like it strong," Mike said.

"Yeah," she gasped, then forced herself to turn and smile at Mike. "Me, too."

He leaned against the door frame, his tall body relaxing as though holding up a building was an everyday task. He'd tucked his right hand into his jeans pocket. The casual gesture hid most of the scars from view. If she hadn't seen it for herself, she'd never know there was anything wrong. Did he spend a lot of time hiding the injury? Don't ask, she told herself. Don't get involved.

"My trailer should be delivered today," she said, sipping the coffee again, trying not to grimace. "I'd planned to go to town and pick up some supplies. Would you like me to get some for you? That is, if your wife wouldn't mind."

"No," said Grady.

"Sure," Mike answered.

She glanced from one to the other. They stood on opposite sides of the large kitchen. It was like trying to watch both players in a tennis match, at the same time. She had to pick one. The choice was easy. She focused on Grady. "No, you don't want groceries, or no, your wife wouldn't mind."

"There's no wife," Mike said.

Grady drew himself up to his full height. "I can answer for myself, boy." He smiled at Jessie. "There's no wife. All those years at sea. A girl in every port. I never had the time."

"No one would take you, you mean," Mike teased.

"I don't see them sniffing around you anymore, either," Grady snapped.

Jessie stiffened. She waited for the explosion, or barring that, the sound of footsteps as Mike stomped away. Instead, the younger man ambled over to the stove and poured himself a cup of coffee. She watched, expecting to see some sign of anger or pain. His gaze met hers; he smiled blandly.

Handsome, she thought again. Sinfully so. Those shoulders alone would insure countless women swooning in his path. But his eyes gave away the secret. Despite the thick, dark-blond lashes and the irises the color of a summer sky, there was nothing inside. No concern, no humor, no hint of a living being. The deep lines bracketing his firm mouth hinted at the pain he'd suffered, but the window to his soul was carefully shuttered.

So Grady couldn't get to him. Interesting. Why was the old man exempt? Were they that close, or was Mike simply immune to Grady's jabs?

"You might want to check the pantry," Mike said, then took a long drink of his coffee. "There's a box of something on the top shelf."

Grady glared at him. "I'm not going to the store."

"Not a problem for me."

"I'd be happy to go, as I said," Jessie offered again.

"I don't give a damn, old man." Mike leaned against the counter. "You're the one going hungry."

"Excuse me," Jessie said, as she stood beside the center island. "Would you two like me to leave? I'd really be just as happy to wait for my trailer outside."

Mike looked at his friend. "Grady?"

Grady pulled his mouth into a straight line. He looked as immoveable as a two-ton bull in the middle of a highway.

"He's a stubborn old coot," Mike said, glancing at her. "I guess that's why he's still here." He looked back at his friend. "When are you going to figure out it's too late?"

With that, he took his cup and escaped out the back door. Jessie stared after him. "Maybe this job isn't a good idea."

"You'll be fine, little lady," Grady said. He gave her a weak smile. "It's him that's the problem. And maybe me. I've been trying to starve him out."

"What?" She couldn't have heard the old man correctly.

"Trying to get him to live his life again. I thought if I didn't keep going into town to buy him food, his belly would force him to make the trip."

"He doesn't leave the ranch?"

"Only to go see one of his doctors. In the last couple of months, he hasn't even done that. He just stays here and broods."

"Why? I know he hurt his hand, but otherwise he seems fine."

Grady's blue eyes narrowed. "You'll have to ask him."

Jessie set her coffee on the counter, then raised her hands in a gesture of surrender. "I'm just the decorator. I don't want to get involved in this."

"The women always like him. No reason to think you'll be any different."

Brandon's face flashed in front of her. There was one very good reason why she was different. She'd loved once in her life, and lost in the most painful way of all. Loving and losing her husband had taught her all about her inadequacies. She didn't need another relationship to highlight them now. There was also a second reason. She wasn't getting involved again. Ever. Losing hurt too much.

But she didn't want to discuss her personal business with Grady. Besides, he wouldn't understand.

She smiled at him. "What's all this about 'little ladies?' We've been women for several years, Grady."

His bushy red eyebrows rose. "Not to me. I grew up saying ladies or girls. On the ship we all said girls."

"I bet that's not all you said."

"Could be." He grinned, then shook his head. "I know about women's rights and all that. I think it's great you have the vote."

"Why, thank you."

"I didn't mean it like that." He looked at her. "You're no push-over."

"Neither are you."

"How long you been decorating hotels and such?"

"About eight years."

"You any good?"

"*You* liked what I sent."

"Maybe I'm not the boss anymore."

She thought about Mike Coburn. The scars on his hand. The pain he refused to acknowledge, yet wore like a badge of honor. "I'm still interested in the job."

"You know how to make pancakes?"

The change of subject made her blink. "From scratch?"

"Nope. That box Mike talked about is pancake mix. Would you mind stirring up a few? I got to go feed the horses."

"Is it that or drive twenty miles to town?"

He nodded."

"Sure, I can make pancakes."

He winked. "It's nice having a girl around the place."

He was still laughing when the back door slammed shut behind him.

The cupboards might be bare at the Coburn-Grady homestead, but the shelves housing cooking utensils were not. Jessie found everything she needed to start breakfast. The box of pancake mix looked old and dusty, but she didn't see anything moving in the white powder and figured there couldn't be anything too awful inside.

She felt as if she'd fallen down Alice's hole and was fumbling through the western version of wonderland. Grady was like an old character actor in a "B" Hollywood western. Mike. She sighed. He was less easy to peg. Maybe a James Dean sort of wounded maverick. The kind of man a woman would give her soul to possess, only to learn he wasn't interested in souls or hearts.

She flipped over the pancakes and reached for a plate. The mix had only required her to add water, but she'd thrown in the egg for good measure. Grady had dug up a sticky bottle of syrup, but there wasn't any butter. Nor did he have fruit or juice to balance the meal. He'd informed her that the garden had yet to start producing, although strawberries would be ready in a couple of weeks.

"That doesn't help us now," she said, as she scooped up three pancakes and stacked them on a plate. She turned, ready to go to the back door and call out that the food was ready, when she heard measured footsteps in the hall.

Mike. She knew before he appeared. It was because he was taller and therefore heavier than Grady, she told herself. Uh huh. There wasn't a scrap of anticipation in her body. No nerve endings sizzled along with the grill. Not a single inch of skin quivered She wasn't fighting the urge to smile. He wasn't her type; geez, she didn't even have a type any more. Nope. She felt nothing.

She sighed. Her mother had always told her she could go to hell for lying, same as stealing. Bad enough to lie to others, but lying to herself was just plain dumb.

"Perfect timing," she said brightly as he stepped into the kitchen. She held out the plate.

"Thanks." He took it with his left hand and moved to the table without once looking at her.

Grady trotted in on his heels and soon the three of them were eating. Silently.

Jessie carefully set down her fork and tried to ignore the lack of conversation. The only sounds were the scrapes of silverware on china and requests to pass the syrup. Since Brandon had died, she'd eaten most of her meals alone, so the quiet shouldn't bother her. But it did. There was enough tension in the room to choke a horse.

Grady kept glancing at Mike, then at her. Mike stared down at his plate. He used his utensils awkwardly, holding the fork in his left hand. She tried not to stare and fought down the urge to offer assistance. She knew better. He would want to do it on his own.

At one point, his finger slipped and the fork went skittering across the table. Jessie grabbed it before it sailed off the side. She offered it to him.

"Thanks," he mumbled, without meeting her eyes. A dark flush crept up his cheeks. Was he angry or embarrassed?

Let it be anger, she thought. That she could handle. It would be easy to stay out of his way. Embarrassment would be lethal, at least to her. She'd always been a sucker for a hard luck case.

Grady retrieved the last of the pancakes from the grill. "Anybody want more?"

"Not for me," she said.

Mike shook his head and pushed his plate away. He'd eaten less than a third of his food. Was it her cooking, or just too much like work to eat?

"I'll clean up, Grady said. "If you two want to go ahead and get started."

"On what?" Mike asked, his voice laced with suspicion.

"Showing Jessie around. She'd going to have to get a feel for what you're trying to do here. I've seen her sketches and all, but you haven't."

"I don't give a damn what she does."

"It's your ranch."

Mike looked at her. "You want to see the place?"

The way he asked the question, he was begging her to say no.

"Sure. If you're not busy."

"Time is about the only thing I do have." He rose to his feet and crossed to the back door.

Jessie paused. Grady gave her a little push. "I might be a bachelor, little lady, but I can scrub a few dishes. Go see what the boss has in mind. We've got to open July first. Can't do that without pictures hanging on the wall."

She walked across the kitchen and out into the morning. Construction workers swarmed over the new building. The last touches were being put on the outside of the guest quarters.

"Looks like they'll be painting the exterior soon," she said when she caught up with Mike. He stood beside the corral and stared at the men.

"Next week, someone told me." He'd stuffed his hands into his jeans pockets. Sometime between their first meeting and breakfast, he'd buttoned up his shirt and tucked it in.

"I understand there are twenty-five rooms in the main building, then ten cabins?"

"Something like that."

"You must be very pleased with the work. It's ahead of schedule."

He glanced down at her. "Isn't it a little late to be selling me on your company?"

"I was just making conversation. Mr. Coburn, if we're going to work together, I think we should have some common ground."

"Mike," he said, then whistled. The black gelding on the far side of the corral trotted over and nuzzled his chest. "Call me Mike."

"All right. Mike. I was just saying that you've got a lovely spot here. I think you'll be very successful."

He stroked the horse's face and neck. "Lady, you don't know what the hell you're talking about."

I will not lose my temper. I will not lose my temper, she told herself. It wasn't working, she thought, but she'd keep trying as long as she could. "You expect to fail?"

"I expect—" He gave the horse a final pat and turned toward the building. "Not a damn thing. You want to see the inside of this or not?"

"Sure."

What was his problem? Was there something specific or did he suffer from terminal jerk syndrome?

Despite her host's attitude, the ranch itself went a long way to uplifting her spirits. For as far as the eye could see, lush wilderness stretched out in all directions. Past the main three-story guest building stood a grove of trees. From the plans she'd read, past the grove of trees, a natural clearing had been seeded with wildflowers. To the right, she saw the first of the individual cabins. Paths had been marked and already men were digging up the earth to plant ground cover. The air smelled clean and alive. Newness and abundance flourished everywhere.

"Just a second," she said, as they walked past her van. She slid open the side door and reached in for her briefcase. After pulling out a large folder and clipboard, she set the case back inside and shut the door. "I might as well take notes."

Mike shrugged, as if it didn't matter to him. She would not, repeat, *not* allow him to spoil her mood.

"Let's see." She flipped through the folder. "Two suites on each of the guest floors. Each of the four corners is a minisuite. The rest are regular rooms, but oversized according to my measurements. Does that sound right?"

"I guess."

"I'm bowled over by your enthusiasm," she muttered, then bit her lip when he glared at her. "Sorry. What else?" She made a great show of studying her notes and stopped watching where they were going.

"Look out," Mike said sharply.

"What?" She glanced up and saw a squirrel run in front of her path. "Oh!" She tried to stop, but her forward momentum made her stumble. The rodent dashed off unhurt as she started to fall. Her papers dropped to the ground.

Mike grabbed her arm. At first nothing happened, then he tightened his grip and drew her upright. Pain shot through her muscles as his fingers clung on to her, digging into her skin. She regained her footing and tried to jerk away.

He released her instantly and stared at his right hand. "The strength. I never know. I didn't mean—"

"I'm okay." She smiled up at him. "Thanks. I should have been watching my step. I'm used to working in the city. We don't have these hazards. I appreciate the help. I always hated skinning my knee."

The place where he'd held her continued to hurt. She would carry a bruise for several days. But she refused to rub the spot or let him know about the pain.

Their eyes met. The man didn't deserve eyes that color, she thought. The shade of summer sky, a joyful color to drown in. They would go unappreciated in his handsome face, overwhelmed by his tall, lean strength.

For a second, the shutters opened and she saw a flash of torment, of confusion. A need so haunting and deep, she feared being sucked inside. Then he blinked and the good-looking but stand-offish stranger returned, leaving her feeling as if she'd peeked through a forbidden keyhole.

"Hey, Jessie. When'd you get here?" a man called as he walked by them. Several one-by-eight boards rested on his shoulders. He broke the spell and she looked away.

"Conrad, hi. Just this morning." She bent down and began to retrieve her papers. Mike joined her. He picked up the sheets individually, using only his left hand.

"You know the crew?" he asked.

"We often work on the same jobs. Although there isn't much overlap. About the time they're done, I'm just beginning." She noticed he was careful to make sure their hands never touched.

She accepted the last sheet from him and rose to her feet. They stepped around the men working on the wide front porch, then moved up the stairs toward the entrance of the guest building.

"My understanding is that the whole first floor is public rooms. Reception area, restaurant, library." She consulted her notes. Grady mentioned something about a glass case. I've ordered it to his specs. Where is it going?"

Mike shoved his hands deep in his pockets. "There's not going to be a glass case."

"Okay, you're the boss." She scribbled his instructions and wondered what she was going to do with the ten foot monstrosity, and who was going to foot the bill. "There was also a rumor of a few antiques being salvaged from the original building."

"In the back." He stepped through the open front door.

She followed him inside. "Wow. This is terrific."

The entrance soared up for two stories. Windows set high on the walls allowed light to pour in. The open space, wood, and glass gave the feeling of letting in the forest. A huge walk-in fireplace dominated the far right wall. Jessie turned slowly, imagining where the reception desk would be, mentally placing chairs and sofas in conversation groups. The bare walls were instantly transformed with prints and paintings by local artists. In her mind, she swept the floor clean of shavings and tools, then scattered brightly colored rugs around.

Plants, she thought, completing her circle and coming to a halt. Ficus trees in the corner. Pots of flowers in the windows. Something tall and delicate on the writing desk. Maybe Mike would consider a ranch dog. She could see the big lumbering animal curled up by the fireplace on a cool evening.

Mike stood just inside the doorway, looking around as if he'd never seen this place before and wasn't impressed at all.

"It's wonderful," she insisted.

He shrugged. "The antiques are through there." He pointed to the long hallway at the back of the room. "First door."

She walked across the floor, carefully stepping over drills and sanders. When she entered the hallway, she opened the door on her left.

"Not that one, he snapped, hurrying after her. "The other one."

But it was too late. Once she stepped inside, she could no more leave than she could stop breathing. Mementos from a military career filled the small storage room. Framed posters of jets covered an entire wall. Model planes sat on a dusty table and took up one corner of the room. On a hook to the left of the door hung a dress white uniform gleaming under the clear plastic of a dry cleaning bag. Jessie reached over and touched the heavy fabric. It rustled slightly. Judging from the width of the jacket's shoulders, it could only belong to one man on this ranch.

In the center of the room, boxes were piled three high. Log books sat on top, and next to them a helmet. She turned to glance at Mike. He stood in the hallway, poised as if to flee. In the dim light, she couldn't see his eyes, but his firm mouth pulled into a straight line. His body stiffened.

"A fighter pilot?" she asked.

"It was a long time ago."

Involuntarily her gaze dropped to his injured right hand. He flinched. Jessie cursed her own insensitivity and glanced around the room, searching for something else to focus on. A small wood and glass box next to the log books caught her attention. She studied the colored ribbons inside.

"Impressive," she said, then moved to the helmet. After setting her papers down, she picked up the helmet and rotated it in her hands. The reflective tape on the back spelled out *Rogue Warrior*. She looked up at him. "You really used to be something."

Three

She'd known him barely two hours and she'd nailed him perfectly.

"Yeah," Mike said slowly. "I used to be something."

The color drained from her face as if she'd just realized what she'd said. He waited for the apology, banked his anger so the explosion would burn them both.

Instead of saying she was sorry, she looked at the helmet. "Was it a plane crash?"

He pushed his hand into his jeans pocket. "No."

"What happened?"

It was none of her damn business. "Some kid stopped to talk behind a jet. The pilot was about to start the damn thing. Instead of letting the kid fry, I pulled him out of the way."

"And?"

"And what do you think?" He pulled his hand out of his pocket and thrust it in front of him. "My reward for a good deed."

She nodded slowly, then glanced back at the helmet. "Rogue Warrior. It suits you."

He started inching down the hall. Inside, pressure built. He had to get away before he exploded.

"It could have been worse," she said, setting the helmet on the box and exiting the room.

"Worse?" He almost laughed.

If he closed his eyes, he would be able to see the hospital room. He didn't have to do much more than that to remember the smells and the sounds. He didn't even have to think to remember the operations, the pain of recovery, the hours of physical therapy, the look on the surgeon's face when he had finally admitted he'd done everything he could. In time—

Mike swore. He hated that phrase. Yeah, in time he would recover seventy percent usage. What was that good for? So far he'd recovered less than fifty.

How could it have been worse? The other pilots—his buddies—couldn't bear to look at him when they'd visited. And the visits themselves had stopped fast enough. Nobody wanted to be reminded of what might happen to them. Besides, there wasn't anything to say. Talking about jets and flights made everyone uncomfortable. For them because they still had the opportunity, and for him because he'd lost his. Everything he'd longed for, everything he'd busted his ass to get, was gone. In an instant, wiped out. No bargaining. No second chance.

"No," he said. "It couldn't have been worse."

She set the helmet on the boxes. "I meant you could have died."

"I know what you meant."

He walked away without looking back. Jessie stepped into the hallway to watch him go. His long strides swallowed the ground. He moved swiftly, with an easy but predatory grace. Only the hand tucked into his jeans pocket hinted at his injury.

Before closing the door behind her, she took one last look at the mementos to the life he'd lost. The ribbons and the uniform were different from her husband's trophies. Brandon had kept photographs of buildings constructed by his company and had proudly displayed his awards. There was a room much like this one, in her San Francisco apartment. A shut-away monument to the past. They were both warriors. Different battlefields, different tokens of victory, similar needs to be the best.

At her feet, a box of photographs lay open. The top two showed Mike with two different but equally attractive women. A rubber band held bundles of cards together next to the pictures. The top one showed a cartoon cat admonishing the receiver to be sure and get well. Obviously Mike had people who cared about him. Why would he say the injury was worse than dying?

Gently, she shut the door behind her. Would Brandon have been any different? Would he have been willing to live his life without his precious buildings? She wanted to say yes, of course, he would have adjusted. She wanted to believe that she—that *their* relationship—would have been enough for him. But she'd long since learned that lying to herself was counterproductive. He wouldn't have lasted a day. The work was the love of his life. She'd come in second. In the end, his true love had killed him.

The guilt settled on her shoulders, the heavy weight as familiar as the coat she wore. Telling herself it wasn't her fault hadn't made her able to shake the feeling. It had been eighteen months since Brandon had died of a heart attack. Eighteen months of her reliving conversations and moments, eighteen months of wondering where she could have made a difference. If only she'd insisted that he eat better and have regular check-ups. If only she'd forced him to take that vacation he'd put off for two years. If only she'd demanded that he not work on weekends.

She leaned against the hallway wall. If only she'd been enough. The truth was she'd never been able to tempt him away from his work. Begging, pleading and black lingerie hadn't budged him. Oh, he'd sworn he loved her more than life. That might have been true. But he hadn't loved her more than his buildings.

Jessie shook her head and forced the memories to scatter. She had a job to do. How ironic that *her* work had become her salvation. It was the only thing left in life she could count on.

Behind her was another door. She opened it and saw the antiques Mike had promised. Chairs had been stacked against one wall. Several small tables balanced on a couple of dressers. Headboards leaned against the window.

Interesting, she thought, taking out a fresh sheet of paper and beginning her inventory list.

Food, her stomach screamed.

Jessie looked up from her seat on the floor of the main room in the guest lodge. The angle of the sunlight through the tall windows told her it was late in the afternoon. Her stomach told her it was very late.

Scattered among the shavings and dust were sketches of individual rooms and swatches of fabric. She tossed the bundle of paint chips to one side. As always, the tools of her work made her feel at peace. Color—bright, soft, loud, warm—it didn't matter as long as it filled her life. Paint might not cure the world's ills, but it sure made rooms more liveable.

She reached for a swatch of fabric in a hunter green print. One of the corner mini-suites looked out onto a grove of trees. She wanted to use wallpaper and paint to bring the feelings of the outdoors in. With this fabric for the bedspread and drapes, and maybe a coordinating, but smaller print on the loveseat and chairs, the room would have a rustic but sophisticated air. She thumbed through her sketch pad until she found the floor plan of the room. After pulling out the list of antiques, she read down until she found the headboard she was looking for.

"Perfect," she said softly, and made a note.

When she was done, she gathered up her samples and rose to her feet. Her legs ached from sitting cross-legged on the hard floor for the better part of the afternoon. Jessie stretched, then bent down and grabbed her coat. The spring day had warmed up into the high sixties.

As she stepped outside of the main lodge, she told herself it was foolish to hope to see Mike Coburn. He would no doubt be avoiding her with the same intensity that a non-swimmer avoided the ocean. She was a bright woman, reasonably articulate, even a successful business person. So why had she consistently put her foot in her mouth? What was there about this place, or that man, that made her so nervous?

She paused at the end of the porch and glanced around the ranch. In the corral, a young man worked a palomino mare. Most of the day laborers had already left for home. The foreman and his assistants, brought in for the job, had retired to their trailers. Conrad had stopped by to tell her that hers had been delivered.

Across from the barn stood the old house. Parts of it, the porch and the front room, appeared to be original nineteenth century construction. The rest had been added on as necessary, creating a hodge-podge architecture that should have been unsightly, but instead charmed and made one feel welcome. Her gaze roamed over the sagging porch and peeling paint. The windows were large enough. Someone had already done a good job remodeling the kitchen. The upstairs bedrooms might be small, but she suspected there were plenty of them so that a couple of walls could be knocked out to provide a big master suite. Maybe before the lodge was done, she would ask Mike if she could take a look around inside and make a couple of sketches.

She pictured the look on his face right before he'd turned and walked away from her. For once those empty eyes had been filled. But with anguish rather than joy. It would probably be best to wait on offering her opinion on remodeling his house.

She crossed the area between the house and corral. Her trailer was on the far side of the barn. For privacy, Conrad had told her. She didn't mind the isolation, she thought as she walked past the house and through the small grove. It would be welcome.

The shiny aluminum trailer stood out like an empty beer can on a pristine white beach. Around the boxy structure, oak trees and pines soared to the heavens. She winced, thinking of the bushes and delicate flowers that had been cut away to make room for this monstrosity. She knew that to build anything new, one often had to destroy the old, but she didn't have to like it.

Jessie reached in her pocket for her key, then unlocked the door. As trailers went, this one wasn't awful. It had been customized for her, and she used it whenever she had an out-of-town job. The front third had been transformed into a work area. A wide drafting table dominated the space. Bookshelves crowded with sample books lined the walls. Squeezed into the remaining two-thirds were a small kitchen and eating area, a bedroom with a queen-sized mattress and dresser, and the bathroom, complete with stall shower. While she worked, she left her TV and VCR at home. Her only concession to the electronic age was a microwave in the kitchen and a portable CD player, along with the case that held her collection.

The customizing had included more than the work area up front. Hooks and small shelves for plants filled every corner. Her plants had been anchored securely in boxes for the trip down. Now she placed them around the trailer. African violets went in a row above the miniature sink. In the bathroom and her bedroom she hung the Boston ferns in lush displays. Cuttings from a cactus plant flourished on the dining table. A pot of geraniums filled the front corner.

She checked the soil and watered the ferns, then gathered the sketches and swatches she'd decided on for the first of the guest rooms. She might as well get her meeting with Mike over with. He was the boss; they would *have* to come to some kind of working relationship.

As she slammed the door shut behind her, she shifted her bundle in her arms. She hadn't been able to escape him all day. Even when she was working, she found her mind wandering to the mysterious Mike Coburn. How had he hurt his hand? Not a plane crash, he'd told her. Pulling some kid out of the way of a jet. The scars didn't look like burns. The thin lines looked more like the remnants of surgery. But for what?

It's just that he's handsome, she told herself. A perfectly natural reaction. It didn't mean anything. It might even be a sign that she was ready to come out of her mourning for Brandon. Not that she wanted to get into a relationship. She'd learned that lesson already. Whatever it took to satisfy a man emotionally, to be enough to be a partner, she didn't have it. Brandon had silently told her that every time he'd left her for work. Every time her pleas that they be together had fallen on deaf ears.

The path from her trailer naturally led to the back door of the house. Jessie strolled along, breathing in the scents of the coming night, enjoying the rustling of the invisible life hiding in the leaves and undergrowth. Somewhere the crickets began to tune up for their nightly symphony. Her boot-clad feet crunched on the dead leaves and twigs.

The path ended abruptly at the rear porch of the house. Light from the kitchen shone through the open windows. She climbed the three stairs to the porch and walked softly to the back door. As she raised her hand to knock, she heard voices.

"It's not my job," Grady said abruptly, from inside the house.

"The hell it isn't," Mike replied.

Jessie stood frozen in place. Should she wait, hoping they'd finish quickly, announce herself, or try for a strategic retreat?

"I can't take care of the house and help you run the ranch," the old man said, stepping into view at the open window. He stood with his back to her. "We need a housekeeper."

Mike swore, the savage word causing Jessie to bite her lip. She inched back toward the stairs.

"I don't want some nosy female here," he said. "Putting herself where she isn't wanted, and generally getting in the way. She'll be more trouble than she's worth."

"Not if you want to keep eating," Grady answered. He pulled out a chair and sat down. Mike paced the length of the kitchen. As Jessie continued to move away from the door, she saw him walk in front of the window, then out of view.

"I don't care about food," Mike said.

"I do. Besides, it's time you stopped hiding from the world."

The sound of the pacing stopped abruptly. Jessie stood poised, one foot on the porch, the other on the top step. Leave now, her mind instructed her. She couldn't. Not yet.

"I'm not hiding," came the measured reply. She would have paid a lot of money to have seen the look on his face as he spoke. "I'm trying to recover. I can't do that with a bunch of people gawking at me."

"From here, it looks a lot like hiding."

"You're just like the rest of them. Wanting something from me. Asking for things. Does your hand hurt? Can I do that for you? Can you come talk to this group of students? What does it feel like to fly an F-14? Can I have your autograph? What are you going to do now that you're washed up?"

He came into view. Both arms hung limply at his side. She couldn't see the right hand, but the left was clenched in a tight fist. His body stood stiffly erect, but he stared at the ground.

"Why can't everyone leave me the hell alone?"

It was like driving by the scene of an accident. She didn't want to look, but couldn't seem to help herself. At last common sense overcame her morbid curiosity. She turned to run down the stairs. But her heel caught on the first step. As she clutched the railing to maintain her balance, her sketch pad and samples flew out of her hands and landed on the stairs with a loud *thump*.

No, she thought, wanting to find the nearest hole and bury herself in it. Please let them not have heard.

It wasn't her lucky day. The back door flew open. "Who's there?" Mike called.

She turned slowly, but couldn't bear to meet his eyes. "Just me. Your resident nosy female coming by to ask your opinion on a few sketches. It can wait."

He didn't answer. The silence stretched between them. Telling herself she deserved whatever happened, she forced herself to raise her gaze.

"I wasn't eavesdropping," she said, as she tried to look apologetic. In return, he glowered.

"I didn't mean you," he said at last.

"Yes you did."

"Yes I did."

"I'm sorry," she said softly. "I do keep falling over myself today. I wish I could tell you why."

His right hand closed slowly into a fist. "Maybe it's me."

With that he turned and walked through the kitchen and out of sight.

Grady appeared at the screen. "He's not going to look at your sketches tonight. You can leave them with me, and I'll give 'em to him in the morning."

"Thanks." She gathered up her work.

"You eat dinner?"

"No."

"You like spaghetti? It's the kind from a box."

She walked to the door and handed him the bundle. When he gestured for her to come inside, she stepped across the threshold. "I don't want to be a bother," she said. "But thanks for the invitation. My trailer has all the comforts of home, but I have to stock the shelves myself and I didn't get a chance to drive into town today."

He glanced at the sketches and whistled softly. "Nice. Which room is this?"

"The second floor east mini-suite." She peered over his shoulder. "It has the view of the tree grove."

"I like this." He pointed at the wall covering. "Not too frilly."

"This is going to be a dude ranch," she said and smiled. "I didn't think frilly would fit in."

"That's right, little lady." The old man grinned. After setting her work on the center island, he headed toward the hallway. "I'll just go get that package of spaghetti."

"Isn't the pantry in there?" She pointed in the opposite direction.

"Yup. But I've been hiding food in my room." He jerked his thumb up toward the ceiling. The eagle tattooed on his arm rippled with the motion. "I wanted Mike to think we were closer to starving than we are."

"Is it working?"

He shrugged. "You heard him, same as me. What do you think?"

"It's not working."

"Yeah. I'm running out of ideas. You might want to look through the cupboards. If we're lucky there's a can of vegetables hiding in one of the corners."

By the time he'd returned, Jessie had finished searching for the promised can. "I can't find anything," she said, closing the last cupboard door.

"Then we're stuck with this." He held up the package.

She pulled out a large pot and began to fill it with water. "I'd kill for a salad."

"Or corn on the cobb." He stared forlornly at the dust box.

"Fresh strawberries." Jessie moaned. "I'll go to town first thing in the morning."

"I'll go with you. We need supplies, and I'm going to hire a housekeeper." He glared at her defiantly, as if expecting an argument.

"I'm not the enemy, Grady."

"I know. It's that boy in there."

"He's not a boy." She adjusted the flame under the pot. Grady sat at one of the chairs by the table. She joined him.

"Maybe that's part of the problem. He's too big to get a whipping. Still he needs some sense knocked into him. He's had plenty of time to get over the accident."

"How long has it been?" The question just popped out. She hoped Grady wouldn't think she was nosy or rude, and more importantly, she hoped he would answer.

"Six months A little more. He spent two months in and out of the hospital, what with the surgeries and all. There's a couple more scheduled, but Mike's about given up hope. It's the flying."

"I guessed that. I saw the storage room."

Grady tossed the package of spaghetti on the table. "Don't let him know that."

"It's too late. He was with me."

The older man leaned back in his chair and laced his fingers behind his head. His plaid cotton work shirt stretched over his barrel chest. "You don't say?"

She shrugged. "It was kind of an accident. He'd told me the antiques were in a room down the hall. I opened the wrong door."

"You've had some first day, haven't you?"

"You could say that." She placed her elbow on the table and rested her head in her hand. "My guess is that he'll fire me in the morning."

Grady's blue eyes narrowed. "Then why'd you work on the sketches?"

"I'm going to do everything I can to make this place as wonderful as it deserves to be."

"Could be Mike's smart enough to keep someone with your enthusiasm around."

"I'm not holding my breath."

"Never a good idea," he agreed, then winked.

She liked Grady, she thought as she rose and walked over to check on the water. "Were you really in the Navy twenty years?"

"A few more than that. I'd been thinking of leaving for a while, but there wasn't anywhere to go. Mike found this ranch and offered me a partnership."

"What did you know about horses?"

"Nothing. But I learned quick. It doesn't take much upstairs to figure out which end bites and which end—" He cleared his throat. "—don't."

She lifted off the cover. The water boiled vigorously. After collecting the package, she ripped it open and dumped the pasta into the pot. The canned sauce went into another pan.

"So you two had always planned on a dude ranch?"

"Yeah. We took it slowly at first, building up the riding stock, then hiring some good cowboys. Finally, we started the construction on the guest house."

"Mike wasn't supposed to be a part of it, was he?"

"Not this soon." The old man rose and began to set the table. "He could have flown for another fifteen years. Maybe longer. He wasn't one of those pilots who wanted to go to work for a commercial airline and earn the money. He was always interested in military jets."

"So it's not that he can't fly?"

"No. He's had his private license for years. With a little more therapy, he could handle the controls." He shook his head. "Horses are fine animals and he's always wanted to own a ranch, but no horse in the world can take the place of an F-14."

"I can't even imagine what it must be like." She stirred the pasta. "Life has a way of surprising us from time to time."

"That's right. You were married to that Ross fellow."

"Brandon."

He leaned against the counter and folded his arms over his chest. "He owned Ross Building and Design."

She nodded.

"You own it now?"

"A sizable chunk."

"So what are you doing out here decorating a dude ranch?"

"I love my work."

Those bright blue eyes saw more than they were supposed to, she thought as Grady held her gaze. His bushy eyebrows, as red as his hair, drew together. "Sounds like there's more to the story than that."

"Okay. I *need* my work. It helps me forget he's gone."

"Your card says Jessie Layton."

"My maiden name."

"You trying to keep it a secret?"

"That Brandon Ross was my husband?"

He nodded.

"Not really. I don't advertise the fact." She picked up the spoon and stirred the pasta again. "He was much older. I didn't really fit in with his friends. I miss him terribly, but I don't miss our lifestyle. It's easier for me to get lost in the work."

"Too bad Mike doesn't have something—or someone—to get lost in." His gaze narrowed.

"Oh, no!" She set the spoon down on the counter and held up her hands in front of her. "Don't even think it."

"What?" he asked innocently. "I didn't say a word."

"You didn't have to. I could tell what you were thinking by the look on your face. The answer is no."

"I don't have any idea what you're talking about."

"Good. Let's keep it that way." She wasn't ready to be anyone's life preserver. She could barely keep her own head above water.

The sauce simmered gently. Jessie picked up a strainer and set it in the sink. "We're about ready here," she said.

"I've got the plates." Grady reached above her to the cupboard and pulled down two.

"What about Mike?" she asked.

"He won't join us."

"How do you know?"

The other man looked older, suddenly, and bent, as if he carried a great weight. "I've seen him get like this. He'll stay in his room for the rest of the evening. Won't eat. He'll be over it by morning." Grady offered her a plate. "I hope."

"He has to eat something."

"You want to make him?"

The challenge surprised her. "Well, why not? What's the worst that can happen?"

Stupid question, she thought as she climbed the stairs toward Mike's room. Any number of things. She reached the landing and adjusted the single rose floating in a squat glass on the tray she carried. It was her contribution to the table setting. Aside from the plain spaghetti, there was a napkin and silverware. No bread, no vegetable, no salad.

"Shopping. Tomorrow," she murmured, then walked to the room Grady had said belonged to Mike and knocked.

Before he could reply, she used her free hand to turn the knob and pushed the door open.

"I brought you dinner," she said, stepping into the room.

He sat at a desk beside the window. As soon as she entered, he released a pencil he'd been holding awkwardly in his left hand and turned over a sheet of paper.

"Oh." She hesitated. "I'm interrupting."

Equal parts of anger and humiliation forced Mike to his feet. "What are you doing here?"

Jessie hovered awkwardly, just inside the door. "I brought you your dinner," she repeated.

He barely glanced at the tray. "I'm not hungry. What business is it of yours if whether or not I eat?"

Her large dark eyes widened. Beside her stood the bed and a night stand. She half turned and set the tray down. After smoothing her hands over her thighs, she looked up.

"None. It's none of my business."

"Damn straight."

With a toss of her head, her thick hair flipped over her shoulders. "Why are you so angry? Is it because Grady cares about you? Is that the crime?"

"Get out!" he shouted, then pounded his left fist on the desk. His pencil rolled to the edge of the desk and dropped onto the floor. The visible reminder of his uselessness, the memory of the uneven, childlike scrawl he'd produced, snapped the last of his patience.

"Lady, I've about had it with you."

"Fine," she said. Her wide mouth pulled into a straight line. "You can try to scare me off this ranch. You can even fire me." She glared at him. "The way things are going, I just might quit. But what are you going to do about Grady? He's stuck here. How long are you going to punish him for what happened to you?"

Her words caught him like a left-right combination to the gut. Guilt and pain were a lethal combination. The woman was reminding him of something he'd been trying to forget: he had been hard on his friend. For the hundredth time he wished he *had* been in a plane crash. At least he would have died a hero's death.

Grady had planned on getting a partner in the ranch. Instead he was left with—

Mike started toward Jessie. She stood her ground. He was forced to reach around her for the leather bomber-style jacket hanging on the back of his door.

"What are you doing?" she asked.

"Going out."

The killing blow occurred when he inhaled the subtle scent of her perfume. It was late in the day. The scent *should* have faded by now. It hadn't. He could smell the sweetly spicy aroma and the underlying heat of her body. It taunted him with needs that were as out of reach as the stars.

He paused long enough to shrug into his jacket.

"What about your dinner?" she asked.

"You eat it."

"But you didn't have any lunch."

Her long straight hair, parted in the center, hung on either side
of her face. He couldn't help himself. Without even wanting to, he
reached out and tucked one side behind her ear.

Soft, like silk. Like a woman's hair should be. Emotions flickered
in her brown eyes.

He moved his hand closer to hold her hair. His scarred, numb
fingers refused to respond. Before he could pull away, she reached
up.

"Don't touch me," he ground out, then pushed past her and out
into the hall.

Four

Mike started the truck and let it idle for several minutes while he
thought about where he was going to go. He was in the middle of
the mountains. His options were pretty limited. Then he realized it
didn't matter. He put the truck in drive and stepped on the gas. Gravel
flew as the tires skidded. The rear of the truck fishtailed wildly. With
his left hand he jerked the steering wheel into the turn and the vehicle
instantly straightened out. He drove to the main road, then headed
for town.

On the twenty mile drive, he only saw one other car and it was
going in the opposite direction. Radio reception was poor, so after
awkwardly fumbling with the dial, he clicked it off. He was left with
the low sound of the motor and his own thoughts.

Images from his past haunted him, flashing through his mind
with the regularity of landing lights. If he concentrated on the pictures, he could hear the low rumble of a jet, feel the ocean swell
beneath his feet and taste the sea spray. He drove on remembering,
the passing scenery little more than a shadowy blur fading to black
outside the glow of his headlights. He stepped harder on the gas,
and the truck sped up. If only it were a jet, he could soar high into
the heavens, nearly close enough to touch the stars. He gripped the
steering wheel tightly.

Instantly pain shot through his right hand. His fingers slipped on
the smooth plastic, the scarred, unresponsive flesh refusing to bend.
The pictures from the past faded. The night grew cold, and he was
alone in the truck going nowhere.

Mike didn't bother fighting the wave of bitterness. He stared straight ahead and got lost in the pain. Only when he'd reached the small town and pulled in front of the lone bar, did he wonder what he was supposed to do now.

Leaving the ranch had been a mistake, but he sure wasn't going back. Grady would be there to lecture him, and that woman. Jessie. He'd seen the pity in her eyes. She'd seen his feeble attempts at writing, and had witnessed his inability to do something as simple as touch a woman's hair.

He leaned back in his seat and closed his eyes. But instead of Jessie's haunted expression, he saw a young man, a kid really, staring at him.

"No," Mike said aloud, not wanting to remember that day, that moment.

The memory refused to budge and he saw it as clearly as it had been almost six months ago. He was still in the hospital, his hand bandaged. The news from the doctor hadn't been good. Tim Evans, the boy responsible for his injury, stood in the center of his hospital room, trying to apologize.

Mike reached his good hand up and rubbed the bridge of his nose, but that didn't erase what had happened that day. No matter how he tried to forget, he could still see the look on Tim's face when he had ordered him out of the room. He'd waved his bandaged hand in the air and yelled that apologies weren't enough to let him fly again.

"I don't need this," Mike said aloud.

The front door of the bar swung open and a couple walked out with their arms around each other. The red and blue neon light flashed on and off, alternately illuminating and hiding them. She was young, blond, and pretty. He looked vaguely familiar. Both in their twenties. Maybe the man worked at the ranch with the construction team. Mike wasn't sure and he didn't care. But in those few seconds when the door had stood open, he'd seen the lights from inside and the crowds of people. A drink might be what he needed.

As he stepped out of the truck, the young couple passed him. Mike glanced at the woman. She looked up and smiled. At one time, Mike would have smiled back without giving it a second thought. Now he turned away and headed for the bar.

Once inside, the loud music and crush of bodies helped make

him feel anonymous. He ordered scotch, straight up, with a beer chaser, then found an empty booth in the corner. He sat with his bad hand next to the wall. On the far side of the room, a dozen or so couples danced to the scratchy sound of a juke box. Mike glanced at them, then looked away when he realized he'd thought one of the women looked like Jessie.

Forget her, he told himself, and downed the shot of scotch. It went down smooth and hot, burning his stomach with a comfortable fire. Forget all of them. Maybe he'd never go back. He'd just sit here and drink until—

"You're in our seat, buddy."

Mike looked up at the large man standing next to the booth. A cheap-looking red-head hung on his arm.

"It's okay, Billy. We'll get another seat," she said, her voice high and wispy, like a child's.

"This is our seat. Move it, mister."

Mike glanced from his beer back to Billy. The other man stood about six four and out-weighed Mike by at least sixty pounds. From the flush on his pudgy cheeks, he was more than a little drunk.

"Make me," he said, then wondered when in God's name he'd gotten suicidal.

"No," the woman groaned.

Billy looked pleased. "What did you say?"

Mike took a long drink of beer and smiled. He slid out of the booth and stood up inches from Billy. "I said 'make me.' "

"You asked for it." Billy drew back his right hand.

Just before everything went black, Mike wondered if Grady would remember to have him buried in his dress whites.

"So there I was. On the wrong side of the island, about to be busted for breaking the law, and me without my pants." Grady paused expectantly.

Jessie forced herself to laugh. "Then what did you do?" she asked, even as her gaze strayed to the clock above the stove. It was after ten. Mike had been gone two hours. Was he all right? It was her fault he'd left in the first place; she knew that. She shouldn't have butted in and said all those things about his relationship with Grady. Besides, who was she to sit judgment on anyone?

"You're worried about him, aren't you?" Grady asked.

"Shouldn't I be? You said he never leaves the ranch."

"Something pushed him over the edge tonight."

"Yeah, me."

He grinned. "I'll say this for you—you work fast. I've been trying for weeks to get him out off the ranch and into town."

Jessie slumped back in her seat. "You should have called me sooner. I'm practically a force of nature."

"He'll be fine."

"But you don't *know* that. He could be hurt or—"

The phone rang. She jumped to her feet. Grady reached up and snagged the receiver. "Hello?"

He was silent for several minutes. She waited impatiently, crossing and uncrossing her arms.

"I know where that is. Yes, I think you did the right thing. No, a doctor isn't necessary. Let him sleep there. Uh huh. Thanks for calling."

Panic and guilt fought it out inside her stomach. Panic won when she heard the word "doctor."

"What's wrong?" she asked as soon as he hung up.

Grady stared thoughtfully at her. "What did you tell the boy?"

Jessie rubbed her hands up and down her thighs. "I don't remember exactly. Just something about him taking his anger and frustration out on other people. Is he hurt?"

"He got in a fight at the local bar."

"A fight? But with his hand, how could he fight?"

Grady grinned. "From the sound of it, the scuffle was pretty one-sided. Mike's beat-up, but he'll survive. I'm going to let him sleep in the bar tonight and go get him in the morning."

"Leave him there?" Jessie drew in a breath and consciously lowered the tone of her voice. "Why? You can't leave him. What if he *is* badly hurt? What if he needs medical attention? What if . . ." She trailed off, realizing she was rambling.

Grady eyed her speculatively. "If you're so worried about him, then you go get him."

"Me? I barely know the man."

"You know him well enough to send him head-first into a brawl."

"A brawl? Oh, don't say that." Jessie bit her lower lip. Why had she interfered? Why was she always trying to fix people? When was she going to learn she wasn't any good at it? "You have to go get him."

Grady leaned back in his chair and placed his folded hands on the kitchen table.

Jessie waited about ten seconds, then headed for the back door. "Is the bar on the main highway?"

"Yup. It's the only one in town. You can't miss it."

"Why do I know I'm going to regret this?" she asked as she stepped out on the porch. But Grady didn't bother answering. He was probably too busy laughing at her, she thought as she pulled her car keys out of her pocket and walked toward her van.

On the entire drive toward town, Jessie told herself to turn around, that she was completely insane and that Mike Coburn wasn't her problem. Then she would remember the raw vulnerability in his eyes when he'd reached out to touch her hair. Stark pain had followed when his hand wouldn't respond to his commands. The fight was her fault. She knew it. She owed him.

She found the bar easily and parked her van in front. It was almost eleven and most of the patrons had already left. Once inside, she spoke to the bartender who eyed her curiously, then showed her to a back room. Amidst cartons of liquor and boxes of napkins, a man lay sprawled out on a cot.

As Jessie entered the small room, she felt for a switch on the wall and flipped it on. He stirred, rolled over and covered his eyes with his arm.

"What the hell do you want?" he mumbled.

"Mike?"

He swore. "Not you. Dear Lord, anyone but you."

She approached cautiously. His blue work shirt hung half-open. It looked like most of the buttons were missing. Dark spots stained the front. With his arm over his eyes, she couldn't see the top half of his face, but the bottom looked battered. His mouth was puffy and red, with a cut on one side and a bruise on the other.

"What happened?"

"You're a bright girl, you figure it out."

Her temper flared, but she reminded herself he was in a lot of pain and that his situation was her fault. "I've come to drive you home."

"Swell." He dropped his arm and slowly sat up.

She gasped. Both his eyes were swollen and bruised. One cheek was puffy and his hands were covered with blood.

"Well, well," he said, reaching up and touching his jaw, then wincing. "You're speechless. It was almost worth it just to witness this historic occasion. I'm not so pretty anymore, am I? Guess the old face matches the hand. Makes me some kind of prize, don't you think?"

"I'm not impressed with your injuries. I had six brothers who all played football. I've seen lots worse than this. I think you're drunk and a fool."

He tried to smile, then caught his breath. He touched the corner of his mouth, then stared at the fresh blood on his finger. "Ow. Nope, I'm not drunk. Only had one drink before Billy wanted his seat back."

"Why didn't you give it to him?" she asked, torn between running to him to offer sympathy, and slapping some sense into him.

"A man likes a good fight now and then."

"Can you walk?"

He looked up at her. "I'm not going anywhere."

"But I want to take you back to the ranch. You need to be cleaned up. Something might be broken."

"It doesn't matter. Why haven't you figured that out?" His words slurred slightly.

"You *are* drunk."

"The bartender did give me something for the pain," he admitted and slowly raised his eyebrows. "Damn." He touched them. "That hurts, too."

"What did he give you? Whiskey?"

He shook his head. "Scotch. Black Label. The best. Only the best." He lifted his right arm. "I got one shot off," he said proudly. "With this hand. Course Billy ducked out of the way, but hell, I made a fist and went for it." He started to slump back toward the cot.

"No you don't." She walked over and sat next to him. "Put your arm around my shoulder. I need you to stand up."

"I don't want to."

"I don't care what you want."

He grumbled, then rested his arm across her shoulder. She gripped his waist, and said, "Stand up." They rose together.

He was heavy against her, and warm. Beneath his shirt, hard muscle rippled with each movement. He was much taller than her, and difficult to keep balanced. "Walk," she said, trying to ignore the way her breast mashed into his side, the scent of him—no cologne, just the fragrance of a man.

She'd forgotten the comfort of holding and being held. For a second, her eyes burned. She wasn't sure why she felt like crying, then she realized that since Brandon had died, she hadn't been this close to a man. Not that this was the least bit romantic, she thought as Mike stumbled suddenly, and she had to hold on tight to keep him upright.

With a minimum of trouble, she got him to the van and buckled him into the passenger seat. She rolled the window down, then closed the door and went around to the driver's side.

When they were more than half-way back to the ranch, she risked glancing over at him. He held himself more stiffly than he had before, and she wondered if the liquor was wearing off.

"How do you feel?" she asked.

"Sore."

"You want to talk about it?"

"Get the hell out of my life."

"You're welcome," she said curtly. "I really appreciate the opportunity to drive on these unfamiliar mountain roads in the middle of the night so that I can come rescue you from your postadolescent behavior."

"Why didn't Grady come instead?"

"He said you should sleep it off there and drive home in the morning."

"He's right."

"I couldn't just leave you there."

Mike stared out the open window. "Why not? Who the hell are you, anyway?"

"I told you. I'm the decorator."

"Then stick to paint and wallpaper, and leave me alone."

"Fine by me." She leaned forward and pushed a tape into the deck. If he wanted to be in a snit, she didn't care. Oh, that wasn't true. Jessie tucked her hair behind her ear and watched the road. They didn't have to be best friends, but she wanted Mike to at least tolerate her. He was in so much turmoil. The sucker side of her wanted to make it all better. Somehow if he would just let himself enjoy the beauty of the ranch, he would . . .

Stop it right now, she told herself. You don't know this man or his troubles. Drop him at the front door, trot back to your trailer and mind your own business.

Her resolve to stay out of his way lasted until she pulled up to the back door of Mike's house. He maneuvered himself off the van's high seat and grimaced as he stepped down. Pain radiated from him, as he slowly made his way to the porch steps and clutched the railing to drag himself to the top.

Jessie watched him take one step. He paused and breathed heavily. She slammed the door shut, then stalked over to him and grabbed him around the waist.

"Leave me alone," he grumbled, but he leaned heavily against her and allowed her to help him inside.

Grady had left the kitchen lights on and a stack of medical supplies on the table, but there was no sign of the old man. Mike pulled out a chair and collapsed into it.

"Aspirin," he muttered. There was a bottle on the table.

Jessie filled a glass with water, handed him two pills and watched him down them. She wasn't sure if she should stay and help, or simply leave him on his own. When Mike reached for a metal bowl and started to get up, she took it from him.

"Do you have to do everything yourself?" she asked walking to the refrigerator and pulling open the freezer door. She dropped a tray of ice into the bowl, then put in some water and set it in front of him.

"I don't need your help."

"Yeah, well, you're going to get it anyway." After dampening a washcloth, she wiped the blood off his left hand, then pushed the raw knuckles into the bowl. "This will help with the swelling."

"Thanks," he muttered through clenched teeth as the icy water stung his open wounds.

"You're welcome." She cleaned up his other hand and went to work on his face.

Mike tried to ignore her. He concentrated on the pain. As the alcohol faded, the hurting cranked up a notch every couple of minutes. Jessie worked carefully, blotting the worst cuts on his face. Concern darkened her eyes to the color of night. Her thick hair swung with her movements.

He couldn't decide if she was a fool or not. Why had she come after him? Was it some misplaced sense of altruism, or simple pity? He fought back a groan. He didn't want to know.

He pulled his left hand out of the ice water and shoved his right one in. The pain wasn't so bad because a lot of his nerves were shot, but the swelling was much worse. Still, he had gotten in that one punch. That was something.

"You should probably take your shirt off," she said, as she rinsed the washcloth in the sink.

Good idea. Before his muscles cramped up and he wouldn't be able to move. He hadn't been this badly beat up since that little incident in Pensacola years before. He shrugged out of his shirt and tossed it on the floor. What had that been about? Something to do with an Admiral's daughter and a guy with a video camera. He grinned. Yup, one of his fellow pilots had caught them on video tape and had threatened to show the reel at the next squad meeting.

"There's more ice," Jessie said, "if you need to— Oh, my Lord."

"What?" He turned to look at her.

She stood by the sink staring at him. Her eyes were big and the color had faded from her face. "Oh, Mike." She walked over to him and crouched down beside him. "Look at what he did to you."

He glanced down. Fist-shaped welts covered his torso. The pattern tightened over his rib cage. It didn't look any worse than it felt. "He got me good."

"I've never seen anything like this. Are you sure you don't need to see a doctor?"

"Yeah. Hey, wait a minute." He drew his eyebrows together. "You said you had six brothers."

She looked up at him, concern pulling her mouth into a straight line. "I lied. I'm an only child."

He could still smell her perfume. The thought came to him unbidden as he inhaled the spicy fragrance. She reached out and gently touched one of the swelling bruises. Her fingers were cool and soft against his skin. Deep inside, in the place he'd thought dead, heat flickered. Nothing to get excited about, he told himself.

She stood up and reached for her washcloth, then began washing the blood from his chest. As she bent toward him, her hair brushed his cheek. A slight turn to get a spot on his shoulder and her breasts paused close to his mouth.

So many curves. He'd always preferred his women long and lean, but there was something appealing about Jessie Layton. His good hand clenched into a fist. Her breasts would spill out of his palm. She leaned over to wipe the back of his neck. Her round rear end would give a man something to hold onto. She wouldn't need a pillow to raise childish hips to the right level. She'd be soft and fragrant and damp and—

He grabbed her wrist. She stared down at him, the washcloth resting on his stomach. "Did I hurt you?"

"No."

"Then what—"

He pulled hard. She lost her balance and tumbled toward him. Her hip landed on his lap. She braced her hands on his shoulders, but didn't push away. Her face was inches from his, and her breasts flattened against his chest.

The stirring inside grew as blood flowed. He hadn't felt a breath of desire since the accident. For the first time in six months, he was hard.

"You married?" he asked.

"No." Something dark flashed through her eyes. "A widow."

He would never have guessed that. So she'd lost something important to her as well. Maybe that was why she knew how to get to him. "You don't seem old enough."

She shrugged. "Even so, it happened. So what is this all about?"

He shifted until her hip dug into his erection. The pressure felt great. "What do you mean?"

"I suspect this entire evening was just some kind of macho stunt," she said, as she tried to pull away.

He wrapped his right arm around her waist and held her fast. "You could be right," he said.

She studied him for several seconds, then nodded as if coming to a conclusion. "For someone who wishes he were dead," she said, "you're going to a lot of trouble to prove you're alive."

Five

He released her instantly.

That had worked especially well, Jessie thought as she pushed off his chest and scrambled to her feet. Not that she hadn't enjoyed being close to Mike Coburn. Even beat-up he was a very attractive specimen of the male gender. She walked over to the sink and rinsed the washcloth, then she tossed it on the counter. If he wanted to clean up, he could finish the job himself.

She started to leave and practically jumped out of her skin. He had silently crept up behind her so that when she turned, she almost bumped into him.

"You like analyzing me, don't you," he said, his voice low and menacing.

"I—" Words stuck in her throat. His blue eyes flashed with pain and something that might have been desire. She read his intentions even before he reached toward her and brushed her hair off her cheek.

"You've been trying to get into my head from the moment you got here," he said.

He traced the line from her ear to her jaw. Shivers raced through her body. She reached behind her and clutched the edge of the counter for support. She had a bad feeling it wasn't going to be enough.

"I didn't mean to upset you," she said, and licked her lower lip.

His gaze followed her movement, then he swept his thumb over her damp mouth. Low in her throat, a soft moan formed. She trapped it there, deciding it wasn't really a problem if she didn't breathe for a little while. Her legs began shaking.

Mike towered over her, a wounded warrior. It wasn't just the scarred hand he carefully kept concealed at his side. It was the bruises on his face, the marks on his broad, tanned chest. Even as she had washed him, she had felt herself drawn to him. Maybe it was because she hadn't been with anyone in the eighteen months since Brandon had passed away. Maybe it was chemical. Maybe it was her own fairly sensual nature finally kicking in after years of being forced into hibernation. Whatever the reason, she couldn't force herself to break free of his gaze.

"This won't fix anything," she said, in a last ditch effort to hold onto some sanity.

He slid his hand under her hair and behind her neck. "This isn't about fixing, it's about forgetting."

"But I don't want to forget any—"

His mouth came down on hers.

Soft, she thought with some surprise, as he gently brushed his lips against hers. Soft and warm and tender. She had expected an assault. He was using her to block out his pain, not from tonight, but from his life. Because of that, she'd expected him to plunge into her with no regard for her feelings.

Instead he whispered and teased at her lips. He mouthed sensual promises, sealing them with a swipe of his tongue at the corner of her mouth.

The hand on the back of her neck squeezed and released, kneading away her tension. She raised her arms and touched his bare shoulders. The heat of him could burn her, she thought hazily. Deep soul burns. Careful of his bruises, she pressed herself against him.

So hard and alive. So different from Brandon, taller, leaner, yet familiar. So very familiar. A man's hardness. The breadth of his shoulders, the flat belly, the ridge in his jeans nestling against the softness of her stomach. Perhaps they were using each other to block the pain.

He reached up and stroked the back of his hand against her cheek. At his urging, she tilted her head and parted her mouth. He brushed his tongue against her lower lips, then slowly entered her. He tasted of whiskey and the night. Tip to tip, they met, circled. Sensations filled her. Her breasts swelled in her bra, her nipples hardened, and between her thighs an ache formed. It had been so long, she had almost forgotten what her body was for. But more than the sensual need, she felt a warmth, a sense of belonging. Holding, being held. She wanted, no needed, more.

As his tongue swept over and around, and the hunger flickered to life, she wondered why this man was the one to awaken her. A few others had tried, but she'd only turned them away. No one had gotten this far.

He raised his head slightly and smiled down at her. He kissed her nose, both eyelids, then her cheeks. He nibbled on her ear. The feel of his hot breath on her neck made her squirm. He chuckled. She looked at him.

"What?" he asked softly.

"That's the first time I've heard you laugh."

He chuckled again. It sounded rusty, but pleasant. She liked hearing him laugh.

He bent down and pulled her even closer. She sensed the change in him and was prepared for the assault. He plunged into her mouth and swept through, a warrior intent on conquest. She arched toward him, prepared to meet him on his terms. She leaned more firmly against him.

He jerked back and winced.

"Oh, I'm sorry," she said, trying not to smile.

"It's not funny," he said, rubbing his ribs.

"I know. I said I'm sorry."

"Yeah, well, you're laughing."

"I am not."

He didn't look convinced. Somewhere in the house, a clock chimed the hour. Suddenly Jessie became aware of herself. She dropped her arms to her sides and stared at the ground.

"It's late," she said.

He stepped away without answering. Part of her wanted him to pull her back against him and make love to her right there in the kitchen. For those few minutes she'd been in his arms, she'd felt more alive than she had since Brandon had died, maybe longer. But he didn't. She glanced around the kitchen, thought about what she should say, then muttered a quick "Good night," and ducked out into the evening.

As she walked away from the house and toward her trailer, she listened to the sounds of the night creatures calling. The temperature had dropped considerably, so she crossed her arms in front of her chest and broke into a jog.

It was only after she was safely inside her trailer and wrapped in a blanket that she allowed herself to think about what had happened. Ignoring the fact that it was tacky to get involved with a client, she reminded herself she was in over her head. Mike was wrestling with some difficult problems and he needed a lot more than she was capable of giving.

Still, the memory of his kiss made her mouth quiver and her thighs tremble as she sat on the edge of the bed. She couldn't deny the attraction. But letting it go any further would be a mistake. No more kissing or touching or anything other than business. She couldn't take the chance. After all, look at how badly she'd failed in her marriage.

* * *

Mike came down the stairs shortly after eight. As he fumbled with his shirt buttons, he found that his normal morning hatred of the world had faded to a steady dislike. If his mouth wasn't so swollen, he might even be tempted to whistle. He cracked a grin, then groaned and touched the cut on his lip. A small price to pay, he thought as he entered the kitchen.

"Morning, Grady," he said, walking over to the coffee pot and pouring himself a cup.

His friend looked up from the paper he was reading. "You look like hell. How's the other guy?"

"I'd like to tell you he looks worse, but I only landed a couple of punches and they were left-handed." Mike moved over to the table and set his coffee down. He picked up the chair, spun it, sat down straddling it and picked up the sports page.

"What happened?" Grady asked suspiciously.

"Nothing, why?"

"You're in a fine mood for someone who got the crap beat out of him."

"I'm always cheerful in the morning. I thought you knew that." He heard a choking sound, but didn't bother looking up from his paper. He wasn't reading the words, he didn't even see them. Instead he saw Jessie's eyes and the way they'd darkened with desire. She'd felt good in his arms, just the way he'd thought she would, all curves and passion. He'd laid awake for over an hour last night enjoying the tightness in his crotch and thinking about kissing her. She'd been sweet and hot and willing and . . .

He grinned and sipped his coffee. His erection was back.

He remembered how she'd clung to him at the end, pressing hard against him. They'd both been without for a while. He set his cup down on the table. A widow, she'd said.

After the way he'd acted yesterday when she'd arrived, she was probably terrified of losing her job. No wonder she'd been so intent on showing him her work. She was young to have buried a husband. He knew several fellow fighter pilots who had died, leaving behind wives and children. Often his friends hadn't bothered to prepare a will, or make financial arrangements. Had that happened to Jessie? He wouldn't be surprised. She was alone, broke, and trying to keep her job so she could pay her bills.

He set the paper down and stared out at the corral. One of the trainers was already working with the horses. In the distance he could hear the construction workers hammering. Mike knew he would have to—

"I'm going into town," Grady said. "I'm going to buy supplies and hire a housekeeper."

Mike's good mood vanished. "The hell you are."

Grady stood up and planted his fists on the table. The eagle on his forearm rippled with the movement of his muscles. He leaned close. "I'm not afraid of you, boyyo. I'm a partner here, and I say we need a housekeeper. I'm tired of starving because you want to hide out from the world."

"I'm not hiding," Mike growled, even as he wondered if the older man was right. But he didn't want to think about it now. He took one more drink of coffee and slammed the cup down. "I'll ride in with you."

Grady paused in the act of pulling on his jacket. He couldn't have looked more surprised if Mike had kicked him.

"I need to get the truck. I left it there last night."

Grady gave him a once over and nodded. "Let's go."

Mike followed him outside. "So why didn't you come get me yourself?" he asked.

Grady grinned. "I thought Jessie could make you feel better than I could." He winked. "I was right, too, wasn't I?"

Jessie tossed the paint chips down and scribbled frantically on the sketch pad. She'd finished her plans for the mini-suites and was starting in on the individual bedrooms. She would then move onto the large suites and finish up with the cabins. There were a thousand details to occupy her mind, but every few minutes she looked up and studied the lush growth around the main lodge.

The crick in her back got worse, so she slid the pad off her lap and stood up. The wooden porch that surrounded the lodge building was still new enough to smell of wood and varnish. She leaned against the railing and watched the horses in the corral. The scent of spring flowers and hay drifted to her. Overhead, the bright green of new leaves diffused the warm afternoon sunlight. She'd long since shrugged out of her jacket. Now she pushed the sleeves of her sweater up to her elbow and tucked her hair behind her ears.

"What are you doing out here?"

She turned toward the voice. Mike stood in the center of the path leading to the lodge. She hadn't heard him approach. "Working," she said, hoping she didn't look as embarrassed as she felt and that the heat on her cheeks wasn't a blush. "It was such a beautiful day, I couldn't stand to be inside."

"That's right. You're the one who likes everything about nature, except crawly things." He took a step closer to her.

In the bright light of day, she could see the bruises and cuts from his fight the previous night. Despite the marks on his face, he looked sinfully handsome and seemed in good spirits. The swelling around his eyes had gone down, although bruises shadowed the tanned skin. He still had a lump on one cheek and a cut by his mouth. But none of that took away from the strong, handsome lines of his profile, or the breadth of his shoulders or the way he swaggered rather than walked. She wanted to ask him to sit next to her and talk about—about anything at all, just so they could get to know each other. But she was afraid of what he would think of her.

She caught her lower lip in her teeth and stared at the porch. Oh, dear, what *must* he think of her?

The silence between them lengthened. Jessie frantically searched for a topic. She saw her sketch pad and bent down to pick it up. "I've made some more drawings," she said. "Do you want to check them out?"

He climbed the two stairs and walked over to where she stood at the railing. As she balanced the large pad of paper, she pointed out the modifications she'd made in the designs.

"I thought it would be better to go more country and less modern. I've checked out most of the rooms. My goal is to bring the outside indoors, and to make the guests' stay more of total experience." She glanced up at him.

He looked from the pages to her. "Uh huh."

"It's not all going to be Early American," she continued, talking faster now. "A couple of the full-sized suites will be country French, and there's an odd shaped room by the stairs on the second floor. I thought of using a Shaker motif there."

Mike shrugged. She noticed he kept his right hand in his jeans pocket. "Whatever."

Oh, he was mister conversation this morning, she thought, fighting the urge to give him a piece of her mind. Why was he standing there like a lump? She should excuse herself, get back to work and forget about him. But she couldn't. Something had happened between them last night. Something wild and wonderful, and as dangerous as it had been, it was something she couldn't forget.

She let the sketch pad slip to the porch. "I spoke to Conrad," she said, trying another tack. "There are several places on the grounds that are going to have to be kid-proofed."

Mike shifted until he was sitting on the railing. He stared over her head toward the mountains. There was a haunted expression on his face, and she wondered what he was thinking about. In deference to the warm afternoon, he'd rolled the sleeves of his white shirt to the elbows. Worn jeans clung to his long legs. His cowboy boots had seen better days. Except for the black watch that looked as if you'd need an engineering degree just to tell the time, he could have been a gentleman farmer or ranch owner out for an afternoon stroll.

Finally he turned his head and looked at her. Deep blue eyes met and held her own. A few strands of blond hair tumbled onto his forehead and she had to clench her hands into fists to keep from reaching out to brush them back. Golly, he sure got to her. Telling herself it had only been a kiss was about as useful as trying to empty the San Francisco Bay with a teaspoon.

"What specifically needs kid-proofing?" he asked.

"Your car, for one."

"The Porche?" He savored that last word, saying it slowly, drawing out the sound as if it were a magic incantation.

She grinned and leaned against an unpainted column. "Yeah, the Porche."

"Hey, don't make fun of my car." He raised one eyebrow. "You ever drive one?"

She shook her head.

"Nothing like it. There's a road that parallels the runway at Miramar. I used to race that baby against one of the jets on take-off." He grinned. It changed his whole face, making his eyes crinkle at the corners and chasing away his faintly hostile air. "Damn near beat the jet more than once."

"Sounds fun."

"The best. Nothing better in the world, except flying, of course."

His smile faded. He folded his arms over his chest, tucking his injured hand out of sight.

"So why don't you fly? Grady said—"

"That old man talks too much."

"He cares about you."

Eyes that had been so warm only moments before became icy and distant. "Stick to decorating."

She should. She told herself she should. Really. "But Grady said you could still fly if you wanted to." She shoved her hands in the back pocket of her jeans and waited for the explosion.

He held her gaze for what felt like forever, then he turned away. "What is the point? You think taking up some little crop-duster is the same as landing an F-14 on a carrier? That a stiff breeze is going to compare to night landings in the rain? You don't know anything."

She sure didn't know when to keep her mouth shut, Jessie told herself. Maybe, assuming she didn't get fired, she could go one entire day without alienating her client. She drew in a deep breath. "So, how do you feel about mauve?"

"Mauve?"

"It's a color," she offered helpfully.

"I knew that, thanks." He sounded sarcastic, but some of the cold faded and he relaxed a little on the railing.

She picked up the sketch pad. "I was thinking of using this wallpaper—" she pointed to the swatch "—and a chair rail, then paint. What do you think?"

"Fine."

"You didn't even look at it."

"I don't care what you do with this place. Paint the whole thing orange for all I care."

She banged the sketch pad on the railing. "Why won't you cooperate with me? This is my job. It's important to me. It must be important to you or you wouldn't have hired me in the first place."

"I didn't hire you," he said. "Grady did. Talk to him."

"But Grady said I had to clear all the decorating with you."

Mike looked surprised. "Why?"

"You're the principle partner."

He stood up abruptly and paced to the end of the porch. "I don't even want to be here."

"I know you'd rather be flying your planes." When he looked up and glared at her, she clutched the pad in front her of, but kept on talking. "It's obvious from everything you've said. But you're not flying planes. You're here. The ranch is wonderful. Beautiful and peaceful. I'm not asking for you to help with the painting or to pick out drapes. Just to look and tell me if you can live with it. Five minutes a day. That's all."

He walked toward her until he towered over her. "You're damn persistent."

She risked a smile. "I know. I want this to work out. Since Brandon, my husband, passed away, this is all I have to keep me sane. I love what I do. Come on, be a nice guy."

Mike shook his head. "No one has ever accused me of being nice."

"You might like it."

"I doubt that." He reached for the sketch pad with his left hand. "What are these?" he asked pointing at her notes in the corner.

"A list of the furniture the room will require. The pieces with an asterisk beside them are already taken care of. Either they're in storage or on order. Everything else has to be purchased."

"It's a long list."

"The room is good sized." She moved closer and pointed. "I've listed the dimensions here."

"How much are you going to have to buy all together?"

She drew her eyebrows together. "I haven't figured it out, exactly. I'll make a master list as soon as I'm done with the sketches and give it to you. There's an antique auction in a few weeks. I'll get most of the stuff there."

"This all seems fine," he said, handing her back the pad.

She took it and clutched it to her chest. She told herself to say thank you and leave before she did or said something stupid. But she didn't want to. She liked him next to her and the way his heat invaded her body, making her remember their closeness of last night.

"How are you feeling?" she asked softly.

"Battered but okay. What about you?"

There was something in the tone of his voice that made her feel uncomfortable. She drew in a deep breath. "Foolish. I'm not usually like that. I haven't, that is to say, since Brandon, there hasn't been anyone . . ." She trailed off. Rather than look at him, She studied the scuffed toes of his boots. "Besides which, you're a client, and that makes whatever happened slightly—"

"You don't know what happened?"

He sounded as if he was smiling, but she didn't risk looking up. "I know that we . . . What I'm saying is that I—" She sighed. "I guess I don't know what I'm saying."

"I do."

"Really?" She risked a glance.

"I was there, Jessie." He flashed her a knowing grin that about sent her to her knees. "What does it matter as long as it gets us through the night?"

He radiated pure male arrogance. Without even closing her eyes she could see him strutting around in his dress white uniform, sending unsuspecting women to their doom all because of that dangerous grin. He was way too smooth for the likes of her.

"They flocked to you, did they?" she asked.

"Women? Sure."

Why not, she thought. He has the looks, had the career. "Herds of the faithful, worshipping at the altar."

"You sound resentful."

"No, just curious. What was in it for them?"

"Then? Bragging right, darlin'." Suddenly, the arrogance slipped away, as visibly as a cape falling to the ground. His expression hardened and his eyes shut her out. "Now? Not a damn thing," he said, then turned and walked down the stairs and onto the path that led to his house.

She stared after him, wondering what she'd reminded him of. Had he been hurt? Abandoned when he was injured?

Unlikely, she thought, crouching down and packing up her supplies. She picked up the paint samples and paused. How many of Brandon's high powered friends would have hung on if he'd been unable to continue running the company? She didn't know the answer, but thought the list might be quite short.

Had that happened to Mike? Is that why he carried around so much pain. She stuffed her pencils into her bag and drew it over her shoulder. Why did he have to get to her so much? Why did it matter what he was feeling? She stood at the railing and watched a squirrel race down the path, then run over and climb a nearby

oak tree. Mike wanted to use her to get him through the night.
Maybe they were supposed to use each other. Did he know how
dangerous that was?

Six

Mike held the rope loosely in his bad hand. He'd managed to get
his thumb in position, and his wrist worked fine. He would master
this, damn it, or die trying. For the hundredth time that morning, he
raised his arm and took aim at the saw-horse positioned in the middle
of the corral. A shirt stuffed with straw served as a make-shift head.
He circled the rope, gauged the distance, and started his throw. At
the last second, his fingers cramped. The thick length caught on his
gloves. Instead of sailing majestically across the ring, it tumbled to
the ground at his feet. He stared at the crumpled pile and wondered
why he bothered.

"I still think it would be worth the trouble to learn to do it left-
handed," Grady said from his place on the fence railing.

"I didn't ask your advice."

"That's true. And you're getting what you paid for."

He bent down and picked up the rope. Left-handed. He stared at
the saw-horse twenty feet away. That would mean he would have to
learn how to throw all over again. But he wasn't getting anywhere
with his bad hand.

Awkwardly he reversed his grip on the rope. He kept his back to
Grady so he wouldn't have to see the little man's I-told-you-so grin.
The morning was pleasant and cool, but Mike could feel sweat drip-
ping down his back. It had nothing to do with the temperature and
everything to do with his effort and frustration. He hated not being
whole.

He raised his left arm. The weight and flow of the coiled length
felt unfamiliar, as if he'd never roped a horse or steer in his life.
Granted it had been years, but he'd never lost his knack. He gauged
the distance and released.

It was worse than with the right hand. The rope tumbled to the
ground like a sick snake.

Behind him he heard Grady's chuckle. "You're not holding it
right, and your follow-through is for—"

"Watch it, old man," he growled as he bent over. "I was roping cattle years before you knew which end did what."

"I'm just saying that . . ."

But Mike didn't hear what his friend was saying because the slight breeze carried with it a familiar spicy scent. He turned and saw Jessie walk toward the corral from the main building. He'd spent the last forty-eight hours avoiding her. It hadn't been that hard. During the day, while she was up at the lodge, he worked with the horses. She went back to her trailer for her meals and worked at her drafting tables in the evenings. He knew; he'd seen her night before last when he'd gone out for a walk. She'd been hunched over the big table, humming tunelessly with some classical CD and drawing with quick, fluid movements.

Everything about her was alive. Her hair, the way it moved as she walked. Her ready smile, the lush curves on her body. Even her clothes. Today she wore a deep blue blouse tucked into black jeans. A brightly patterned vest, left unbuttoned, emphasized her generous bust line. Dangling earrings glinted with each step. He'd never seen her in a dull color.

When she reached the railing, she spoke quietly to Grady before turning her attention on him. "Morning."

He grunted in return and turned away. After collecting the rope, he tried to get his left arm to rotate properly. Even uninjured, it felt awkward. Frustrated, he dropped his arm to his side and turned to her. "What do you want?"

She took a step back. Dark eyes met his. "I was taking a break," she said. "If I'm bothering you, I can leave."

"Don't mind him," Grady said, patting the railing next to him. "He loves to perform for an audience, don't you?"

Mike didn't answer.

"I remember the time three senators and some official from NATO came on board the carrier. It was a clear day, but the angle of the wind was off. Nobody wanted to do the carrier landing because there were more than even odds they'd have to bolt because of a wind sheer. Now our boy, Mike, he jumped at the chance."

Mike turned his back on them and tried to close out the memory. Even as he circled the rope again and again, he could feel the salty ocean breeze slap his face and hear his RIO's concerns.

"We can't mess this up," he'd said. "That senator is from my home state. The news people are local. My mama is going to be watching me on TV."

"Don't sweat it," Mike had answered as he'd climbed into the cockpit. "We'll ace it."

And they had. A perfect carrier landing. The double-thunk of the wheels hitting the deck and the tailhook picking up the cable was instantly followed by the bone-slamming crunch of the F-14 being jerked to a halt. He'd made CNN that day.

He released the rope. This time it sailed toward the saw horse, but fell short of the stuffed head by about five feet.

"Good," Grady called. "Use your wrist."

He swore at the old man under his breath and did his best to ignore Jessie, but he kept catching glimpses of her out of the corner of his eye. She sat on the railing. Her boots gleamed in the sunlight. They were a rich brown with hints of red, almost the color of her hair. Now she was laughing at something Grady was saying. The sweet sound carried to him on the same breeze that taunted him with her perfume.

It had been a long time since he'd wanted a woman. Even longer since he had to think about whether or not he could get one. He pulled the rope and coiled it up. As he raised his arms, he remembered how women had always approached him. His lines were so smooth and practiced, he didn't even have to think about them. As the rope sailed toward the saw-horse, he remembered a particular leggy brunette had wanted to touch his medals while they were in bed. Another had asked him to let her wear his hat while she rode him. The brim had bounced and slipped with each passion-induced thrust of her hips. The rope caught the stuffed head, but slipped off the side.

"Better," Grady called.

Mike ignored him. He lifted his Stetson, wiped the sweat off his forehead, then placed the hat back on his head. He could feel Jessie watching him. He concentrated on the rope and the saw-horse. But instead of Jessie's soft laugh and Grady's familiar voice, he heard the roar of the millions who had lined the streets of New York during the parade after the Gulf War. He remembered Pam waiting for him in his hotel when he returned.

Pam. He released the rope. This time it landed cleanly over the saw-horse. Jessie applauded and Grady whistled. He didn't acknowledge them. It had been almost six months since he'd seen her.

The past flooded him with sensation until the dusty corral disappeared and he was back in the hospital, back in constant pain, raging against the fate that kept him from flying.

Pam had visited him twice. The first time she'd been the caring girlfriend, confident he would recover. With her pale blond hair and elegant good looks, she made her living modeling lingerie for a popular catalog. They'd talked about their future, because he hadn't been man enough to tell her the truth. That there was no future, that he would never fly again, that the Navy was going to let him go. He'd known what would happen when he told Pam. Despite the two years they'd spent together, she would walk away without once looking back. She'd made it clear from the beginning—she was interested in a fighter pilot. A fair exchange; he'd wanted a fashion model. Love, fidelity, or even affection didn't enter into their agreement. He didn't know what she did when she was away from him, and he didn't ask. She returned the favor.

He released the rope, and for the second time it sailed cleanly through the air and landed on the saw-horse. This time when he coiled it up, he changed position in the ring.

In the end Pam had heard the truth from one of his buddies. She'd visited him that night to tell him it was over. She'd been beautiful and perfect, as always, but the pain in his chest hadn't been about losing her. Instead, her defection had brought home the hardest truth of all. Without his wings he was no one. Just a shell of a creature, alive, but not living. In that single moment, when her green eyes had stared down at him, he'd seen the flash of irritation followed by pity. She'd kissed him on the forehead, as if he were her grandfather. No, he thought, shaking his head. As if he wasn't a man anymore.

Jessie laughed again. He glanced over at her. She clutched the railing with both hands and tilted her head back. Her action exposed the long line of her throat. The sun highlighted the warm color of her skin. She would tan easily, her skin turning a rich, deep brown. He wondered what color the palest parts of her were. Pam had been milky white, but he'd bet Jessie would be more like rich cream, tinted with a hint of color.

She looked at him and their eyes met. Something flashed between them. Something hot and electric. Suddenly he could taste her again.

As his gloved fingers curled into his palms, he felt her soft body beneath his. He caught his breath, then exhaled it slowly. The sharp pain in his injured hand didn't bother him. She made him feel whole again.

"Maybe you could teach me to throw a rope," she said. "Of course, I have terrible aim."

He shrugged as if he wasn't especially interested, but he pictured her in the ring, laughing with him, teasing him with her scent.

"If he doesn't want to teach you, little lady, I will," Grady offered.

Before Mike could argue with his friend, a car came around the lodge and parked in front of the house. The vehicle was a smallish import, about five years old. A sensible car. Mike dropped the rope and started walking to the edge of the corral. Grady and Jessie had already scrambled down.

The car door opened and a woman stepped out. She was about five foot eight, with graying brown hair pulled back in a bun. She wore a cotton dress and the ugliest shoes Mike had ever seen. She glanced at the three of them. Piercing brown eyes studied them.

"I'm looking for a Mr. Grady," she said.

"That would be me." Grady stepped forward. "You must be Mrs. McGregor."

Mike glared at his friend, but Grady was too busy shaking the woman's hand. He knew why she was here even before Grady gave him a wink.

"Mrs. McGregor is our new housekeeper."

The older woman nodded, then moved to the trunk of her car and popped it open. "I'd best be getting started. You said you wanted me to cook the evening meal. I'll need to know your preferences."

Grady smiled so wide, Mike thought he might split his face in two. "Be happy to. Mike? You want to come in and tell this fine woman what you'd like for dinner tonight?"

He'd agreed to a housekeeper because it was easier than fighting with Grady. Or starving, he admitted to himself. But he didn't have to like it or cooperate.

"I can't right now." When Grady looked like he was about to protest, Mike silenced him the only way he knew how. "I promised Jessie I'd introduce her to a couple of the horses.

Jessie glanced up at him. She was surprised at the offhanded invitation, but she didn't let on to Grady.

If possible, Grady looked even more pleased. "So what's stopping you then?" He grabbed several bags of groceries from Mrs. McGregor's trunk and headed for the house. The new housekeeper followed.

When they were alone Jessie said, "I really would like to see the horses, if you have a minute."

"Why not." He owed her for going along with him.

Jessie walked along side Mike as they went toward the barn. "You did well with the rope," she said.

He grunted.

She sighed. So he'd used up all his conversation already today. Too bad. She'd missed seeing him around. Despite all the work she'd been doing in the last couple of days, she still found the time to feel lonely.

They entered the stable. She inhaled the fragrances of hay and horses. Everything smelled clean and not nearly as overpowering as she'd thought.

"Here they are," he said, motioning to the stalls lining the walls. Several horses poked their heads over the doors and stared at her.

"I'm going to groom a couple of the mares," he said. "Do you want to help?"

Was he inviting her to stay? Just like that? Instantly her spirits lifted. Maybe he didn't dislike her as much as she feared. She shoved her hands into her back pockets. "Sure. If you don't mind me being here. I don't know anything about horses. I was on a pony once, when I was little, but that was about it."

"You can't expect to decorate a dude ranch if you don't know anything about horses," he said.

He was smiling at her. Jessie grinned in return. "You're right. What do you want me to do?"

"There are a couple of new mares. The best way to make friends with a horse is to spend a little time with her. So we're going to introduce ourselves and make the two of them look like they're pretty enough to go to church."

He led a bay mare out of one stall and a palomino out of another. After showing Jessie the brushes, combs and cloths, he let her pick her horse. She chose the little bay mare.

"Her name is Missy," he said.

"Hi, Missy."

She watched Mike speak softly to his horse. When he picked up a large brush, she followed suit. The horses were about four feet apart, tied up to the stable wall. A cool breeze blew through the open doors at the front and back of the building. She stroked steadily, brushing away dust and making the animal's coat smooth again. Every few minutes she looked up and watched Mike at work.

"This is nice," she said. "Kind of relaxing."

"Wait until your shoulders start aching."

She noticed he worked mostly with his left hand. Occasionally he fumbled with the brush, but instead of getting angry, he tightened his grip and kept on brushing. He'd taken off his gloves. Even with his injury, his touch was sure and loving. He might hate the ranch and resent being here, but he loved the horses.

"For some jet jockey, you sure look like you know what you're doing with that horse," she said.

"I used to live in Oklahoma. I grew up on a ranch."

That was a surprise. "So how did you get from there to the Navy flying jets?"

"There was an airstrip just a mile or so from the far end of our land. I used to spend all my time there. I learned to fly when I was about thirteen. The next year, I went to my first air show and saw some military jets. I was hooked." He moved to the other side of his horse and she did the same. Now instead of being able to see him, they worked back to back.

"Why the Navy? Why not the Air Force?"

"I wanted to be on an aircraft carrier."

She glanced at him over her shoulder. "You *wanted* to spend months at sea?"

"It's not so bad. Although the carrier does lack certain essentials."

"Let me guess. Women." She leaned against Missy and admired the play of muscles in Mike's shoulders and back. Her gaze lowered to his tight rear end encased in worn jeans. He took her breath away and her fingers ached to touch him. The rush of sensual need caught her off guard and she quickly began brushing the mare.

He turned to her. She continued to work and prayed she wasn't blushing. He'd pushed his hat back far enough that she could see his blue eyes. They were an impossible color and should be declared illegal. His bruises had faded to smudges, deepening the hollows of his cheeks and outlining his jaw.

"It wasn't just about sex," he said.

"Oh, sure. You missed the stimulating conversation you had with all your women."

A grin slowly stretched across his mouth. *"All* my women? That's quite an assumption."

She almost said, "That's because you're quite a man." Almost. But she didn't. "So what did you miss about women other than sex?" she asked, then wondered why she was foolish enough to be having this conversation in the first place.

"Their smell."

She stopped brushing Missy and looked at him. "Their what?"

"Women smell different than men. Mostly it's perfume, but it's something else as well. After being at sea all those tours, I've become sensitized to a woman's scent."

Jessie fought the urge to sniff her forearm. "I didn't know that."

"You smell very nice."

Now she *knew* she was blushing. She turned back to her horse and brushed vigorously. "Thanks. I still don't understand why you chose the Navy. Carrier landings would have to be pretty exciting for me to live on one of those ships for six months at a time."

"I met some Navy pilots first," he answered. "I thought they were gods."

"And you wanted to be worshipped?"

"That I did."

She laughed. He didn't join her. She looked at him over her shoulder. "You're not kidding."

He set the brush on the wooden table next to the wall. "It's hard for me to explain, but being a pilot is a lot more than a job. It's a way of life. Because of what we do, and the difficult training we go through, we form a bond with each other. Because we are . . ." He hesitated, pausing to find the right word.

"Warriors?" she offered.

"Yes, warriors. People look at us differently."

"Were you ever afraid?"

"No." He took off his hat and dropped it on the table, then he rubbed his hand across his forehead. "There's nothing to be frightened of. Flying a jet is digital. A one or a zero. You either come back alive, or you don't come back. Almost no one walks away from a crash." He shrugged. "I knew I wouldn't crash."

"What about your hand?" she asked, then could have kicked herself when he immediately shut down. The friendly gleam in his eye faded. He picked up a different brush and moved to the far side of his horse.

"That was a mistake," he said, without looking at her. "It didn't happen in a jet."

Silence. Jessie petted the bay mare and wished she'd kept her mouth shut. They'd been doing so well. Mike had opened up to her, and she'd blown it.

Now that she'd had a peek into his world, she was beginning to understand his frustration. Brandon would have rather died than live without his work. Even if he'd known it was going to kill him, he would have kept on doing it right up to the end.

It had killed him, she thought glumly. Nothing she'd been able to say or do had dissuaded him from his need to work constantly.

She could feel Mike's tension. Frantically, she searched her mind for another topic of conversation.

"It's only two months until the dude ranch opens. You must be very excited."

He grunted.

She turned to face him. "Well, damn it, I'm sorry. Okay? I didn't mean to mention your hand. I made a mistake. I put my foot in my mouth. You should be used to it by now. If you didn't want to talk to me, why did you invite me to join you?"

He didn't bother looking at her. "An error in judgment."

"Just like buying the ranch was an error in judgment."

"I wanted the ranch," he admitted.

"Just not now," she said. "Not like this." This time she said it deliberately and dared him to get angry. She was ready to give as good as she got. But instead of seeing him stiffen in anger, he seemed to fold in on himself.

"Not like this," he agreed.

"Oh, Mike." She took a step toward him. Suddenly, something butted her back. She took another step forward, but she was off balance and started to go down. Mike saw and ducked

under his horse's head to make a grab for her. He stepped on the
brush she'd dropped, lost his footing and tumbled into the straw on
top of her.

Seven

"You did that on purpose," she said, glaring up at him.

Her face was inches from his and her sweet breath fanned his
face. He braced his hands on either side of her head and started to
push up. Only then did he realize he was lying directly on top of
her, one of his thighs nestled between her legs and his chest hovering
just above her full breasts. The position had possibilities.

"Why would you think that?" he asked softly.

"Why? Just look at us."

There was a bit of straw in her hair. He reached up with his left
hand and pulled it free. Then he touched the loose strands. His breath
caught in his throat. As soft and silky as he'd imagined. He tightened
his grip on her hair.

"M-mike?"

Their eyes met. He saw the desire flickering in her dark irises,
but he also saw something more. Apprehension. She was unsure of
herself.

The realization caught him off-guard. He'd only ever known beautiful, confident women. Women who were comfortable with their
attractiveness and knew how to use it. Jessie, with her generous
curves and teasing humor, was different from them, but no less appealing. Apparently, she didn't know that.

Her arms were at her sides. Her hands picked at the straw under-
neath them. She didn't try to push him away.

He thought about using one of his lines. The smooth, practiced
statements usually flowed like water when he had a woman in his
arms, but it had been a long time for him. Besides, he didn't want
Jessie to hear his lines. He wasn't sure why; it just didn't feel right.

"Are you going to let me up?" she asked.

"Do you want me to? I'm enjoying this."

"Well, I can't breathe."

He wasn't even touching her chest, so he knew she was lying,
but he rolled off her all the same. Before she could scramble to her

feet, he slipped his left arm around her waist and tugged until she was on her side facing him. A strand of her hair slipped across her cheek. He tucked it behind her ear.

They were so close he could see the flecks of gold in her brown eyes. Her full mouth parted slightly, as if she needed more air. Her hands were between them, balled up into fists. Slowly, so slowly he thought he might go mad before she was done, she uncurled her fingers and pressed her palms against his chest. Her heat seared him. He bent forward and touched his lips to hers.

It was more than passion, he thought hazily, touching her mouth gently, brushing back and forth before pressing harder against her. More than need. He drew the tip of his tongue across the fullness of her lower lip. She arched against him, her soft stomach coming to rest against his pelvis, her legs tangling with his. It was about finding a place to forget.

He reached around and pulled her closer still, so close that her breasts flattened against his chest. She raised her hands to his shoulders, then touched his face. Her warm fingers stroked his cheeks, traced his eyebrows, circled past his ears to get lost in his hair.

She opened her mouth to him. He dipped inside and tasted her sweetness. She felt hotter there, and the heat found its way to his soul. His own blood rushed faster, his heart pounded. His jeans grew tight. He welcomed the ache between his thighs and wanted to bury that part of him in her. All lush curves, so connected to the earth, she was a haven to him. Not for healing—he was past that kind of redemption. Instead, she provided a place to escape.

Her tongue met his own. She performed none of the intricate dances Pam knew. If anything her responses were timid and untutored. But when he nibbled her lower lip and made her moan deep in her throat, he wanted her more than he'd ever wanted another woman. He swept around her mouth, teasing her with sensation. She followed his lead, sending ripples of hunger surging through his body.

He pulled back and looked at her. With her eyes closed and her cheeks flushed with color, she looked wanton and sexy enough to threaten his control.

"Ah, Jessie," he murmured, then pressed against her shoulder. "You are so damn beautiful."

Slowly, she rolled onto her back. She blinked slowly and looked up at him. Her hands never left him. She continued to touch his chest, then stroked his arms. When she reached for his hands, he moved back and straddled her.

His crotch nestled intimately with hers. Heat transferred and his erection surged against the fly of his jeans. Their eyes met. She held his gaze, then turned away, obviously embarrassed. A little of her apprehension had returned, just enough to take the edge off her passion.

"Why don't you believe you're attractive?" he asked.

"Because I'm not."

"You couldn't be more wrong." He was going to prove it to her, too. He reached for the first button on her blouse.

His right hand refused to cooperate. His left fumbled with the tiny buttons, but he couldn't manipulate them through the holes. He tried several times before he realized the task was impossible. He wasn't enough of a man to undress her.

He felt as if he'd been plunged into an icy stream. His passion faded as frustration and humiliation swept over him. He stood up and turned away.

He cursed silently, wanting to pound his useless hand into a bloody stump. He leaned against the palomino mare and prayed Jessie would just leave him be. He could feel the rage threatening, and for the first time since he'd met her, he didn't want to take his temper out on her. He wanted to crawl away and never see her again, but he didn't want to hurt her.

The mare nibbled at his shoulder. He ignored her. He tried to swallow, but his throat felt dry. Funny, he thought without humor, that this hurt more than Pam's leaving. Maybe because he'd always known the rules with Pam, and now everything was different because he was different. Less than a man.

"Mike?"

"Go away."

"Mike, I—" She paused. "Mike?"

"Damn it, Jessie." He spun on his heel. "Can you leave me—" He stared at her, not able to believe his eyes.

She knelt in the straw, facing him. Her chin tilted up defiantly. While his back had been turned, she'd removed her vest and blouse. And her bra. She was naked from the waist up.

"Jessie?"

Dark eyes met and held his. He searched her gaze for pity and found none. A shiver raced through her and he realized she was trembling. If her eyes didn't lie, it was from fear and need. "Touch me, Mike. Please."

"Jessie." This time he said her name like a prayer. He crouched down beside her, not daring to caress the perfect shoulders or generous breasts she'd bared for him.

Passion returned to him, and with it, something more. A deep need to make her understand how much he appreciated her gift.

"Sweet Jessie." He spread out her shirt, then lowered her onto the soft cloth.

"I don't want you to think I'm easy," she whispered.

He smiled. "I knew that."

"I don't mind about your hand."

He didn't want to think about his handicap. Not now. "Forget it," he murmured, stretching out beside her and reverently resting his left hand on her stomach. Beneath his palm, her warm skin quivered.

"You're so perfect," he said, looking at her chest. The morning sunlight made her olive skin glow. Her breasts moved with each breath she took. Dark nipples pointed up toward him and he couldn't resist tasting her.

He bent his head down and drew the soft nub into his mouth. As he sucked gently, the sensitive flesh puckered. He circled the small tip with his tongue until it hardened and Jessie arched toward him. She clutched his shoulders and whispered his name.

He repeated his ministrations on her other breast. Then he cupped her breast in his left hand and squeezed the fullness, liking the way it filled his palm. So different, yet so right. He kissed her again. The need surged inside of him. He wanted to claim her as his. He wanted to bury himself in her waiting warmth and feel her slick feminine shape close around him. He wanted to plunge in deep, then pull back, making them both pant with anticipation. Not yet, he thought, trailing kisses from her jaw to her ear before sucking on her lobe. Soon. Very soon he would claim her and mark her as his.

He breathed into her ear and heard her giggle.

"Stop. That tickles," she said, squirming.

He blew again, then turned his head so he could watch her breasts bounce as she laughed. He leaned down and took one hard nipple in his mouth. He used his left hand to play with the other breast. He tended to her, kissing and nibbling and flicking his fingers, and pulling and sucking until her breathing came in quick pants and perspiration coated her chest. Only then did he raise his head and look at her.

Passion glazed her brown eyes and her body quivered with anticipation. Soon, he thought, and gently kissed her mouth.

He lay next to her, soothing her with quiet words. When both their pulses had returned to normal, she rolled over to face him. She tried to smile, but the curve of her lips faded into a straight line. He read the concern in her eyes and it moved him as nothing had in months.

"I told you you were beautiful," he said, touching her cheek.

"I'm so confused."

"Why?" he asked. "Because I want you? Is that so strange?"

"So it's about sex?" she asked, sitting up.

He smiled. "Oh, yeah."

"Have you been with anyone since the accident?"

His smile faded. "What does that have to do with anything?"

She put on her bra and pulled on her shirt. Quickly, she fastened the buttons and stuffed the tails into her jeans. Even with her clothes on, she still looked tousled. The passion lurking under the surface flared to life. He banked the fire and knew his time would come.

As she drew on her vest she said, "I haven't been with anyone since Brandon died. I went on one dates six months ago, but it was so awful, I haven't been out with a man since. We're both on the rebound from a tragedy in our lives. Have you considered this is just a reaction to that? We could be making a big mistake."

He didn't want to think about anything any more. He was damn tired of thinking. Of weighing the consequences of his actions. He just wanted to forget. To get lost inside of something other than himself.

"Mike, this could all explode in our faces. I don't want that to happen. We've both been hurt enough."

He could have handled his flash of emotion if she hadn't glanced at his hand just then. He sprang to his feet. Minutes ago, he'd fought desperately not to hurt her. Now he wanted to lash out and make her bleed like he was bleeding.

"It was just a roll in the hay, Jessie," he said. "Literally. Don't make it more than it was." He headed out of the barn and didn't bother looking back.

Jessie stared at the swatches of wallpaper she'd taped to the main dining room. She'd narrowed her choices down to three. Normally she would bring in her client and have him make the final choice. But that would mean talking to Mike, and she'd been avoiding him for almost a week.

Seven days, she thought as she paced the long empty room in the lodge. More importantly, seven nights lying alone in her trailer staring at the ceiling. But instead of the darkness, she'd seen the look on his face when he'd turned in the barn and saw her sitting bare-breasted before him. She'd never done anything like that before in her life. But if she lived to be a thousand, she would never forget the look in his eyes when he'd reached for the buttons on her blouse and had been unable to open them. The shame and impotence in his expression had touched her heart, stirring to life compassion and a desire to help him. Coupled with her own passion, the impulsive decision had been easy to make. Until he'd turned and looked at her.

Jessie stopped in the middle of the room and glanced out one of the big windows toward the forest. In that second, he could have crushed her with a flippant word. Instead, he'd stared at her with the reverence of a saint staring at the heavens. He had told her she was beautiful and, held and touched by him, she had risked believing.

Even thinking about his gentle hands and mouth on her made her body tingle and her breasts ache for him. She had dared to think he was coming around. She shoved her hands into her pockets and resumed pacing in the room. She couldn't have been more wrong.

Just a roll in the hay. The words echoed again and again in her mind. She didn't matter to him. Any willing female would have done. She was simply an available but interchangeable part.

"So forget about him and do your job," she told herself, speaking aloud.

But she couldn't forget. She'd seen the need inside him. Not just for sex, but for something else. A healing. And she'd never been able to turn her back on someone who needed her. Even when she knew she couldn't make a bit of difference. Even when she knew the darkness in his soul was beyond her. Even when he didn't want her help.

She stomped her foot on the bare wood floor. It felt good, so she did it again. Gathering her resolve around her like a shield, she took one last look at the samples of wallpaper she'd taped up and headed outside.

Spring had come to the ranch and the temperature was in the mid seventies. Flowers bloomed everywhere, and birds and small animals rustled in the new growth.

When Jessie stepped off the porch of the lodge, she could see the main corral. Mike worked a black horse on the end of a lead. The skittish animal had been delivered a week ago. From different rooms in the lodge she'd seen him working with the animal every day. Today he trotted it around with a blanket on its back.

Jessie approached slowly. She pulled her hands out of her pockets, then stuffed them in again. Mike had taken off his hat and the sun glinted off his blond hair. It would be so much easier if he wasn't so good-looking. And tall. She watched the play of his muscles as he moved with the horse, turning in the center of the ring, while the animal trotted along the outside.

When she reached the railing, she leaned against the wooden corral and watched him. He turned and saw her. Not by a flicker of a lash, did he give anything away. She couldn't tell if he was happy to see her or wishing she had crawled under a rock and died. His only acknowledgment of her presence was the way he slowly pulled the horse closer to him. With each circle, he drew in the line until the animal stopped in front of him.

"Good boy," he said, patting his head and neck. "Good job."

She liked how gentle he was with the horses. She was a sucker and a fool, but his attitude toward them gave her hope. He hadn't shut down completely. Brandon had never taken the time to deal with anything but his work. It would never have occurred to him to care about an animal.

"He's coming along well," she said, as Mike approached.

Mike nodded.

Golly, this was going to be easy. "I have some wallpaper samples taped up in the dining room. I'd like you to come and take a look at them and pick the one you like best."

He tied the gelding to the rail and ducked through. When he was standing in front of her, he pulled a handkerchief out of his front pocket and wiped his face, then tucked the cloth back in his pocket. "You decide."

"But I can't make up my mind. I need your help." She was pushing him and she knew it, but she didn't know any other way to try and make things right between them.

He stared at her. She wanted to turn away, but she forced herself to hold his gaze. The calm facade of his expression cracked slightly and she caught a hint of regret.

He pulled off his left glove and touched her cheek. "I'm sorry," he said. "You surprised me. Hell, I surprised myself. I didn't think I could—" He dropped his hand to his side. "I was a real jerk. I didn't mean to hurt you."

"Really?" She fought against the happiness that filled her, then decided to just let herself revel in it. Hadn't she come out here to make her peace with Mike? She rocked onto the balls of her feet, then back onto her heels. "You're really sorry?"

"Don't push it," he growled playfully.

"Okay." She smiled. "I forgive you."

He shook his head. "As easy as that?"

"Sure. Why not?"

"You don't believe in holding a grudge?"

"It takes too much energy. But if it makes you feel any better, why don't you come and look at the wallpaper and then we'll call it even."

He hesitated and she thought he was going to turn back into his normal gruff self. Instead he looked at her and grinned. "You don't give up, do you?"

"Never." She took a step toward the main building. "Come on. It will only take a minute."

"All right." He grabbed his Stetson off the railing and called for one of the men to come and take care of the horse.

"I've been leaning toward a restful color for the dining room," she said, as they walked through the dirt. "There's going to be so much activity during the day, I thought that might be a nice change."

"Uh huh."

"I'm not too sure about a chair rail, though. I think they can be over done." She chatted on until she realized he wasn't paying attention to her, but was instead checking out the construction on the individual cabins.

She slowed. "They're making a lot of progress. You must be pleased."

"Surprised is more like it."

"Because the work is going so well, or because you didn't expect to be here right now?"

He stopped. "You don't bother being subtle, do you?"

"I've tried, but it's not something I do very well."

"I can believe that." One corner of his mouth twisted up slightly. "You're right. I didn't expect to retire from the Navy for about fifteen or twenty more years."

"It's still very beautiful here."

"For a prison." He looked past her toward the mountains, in the direction of the sea. What was he looking for?

"It's only a prison if you choose to make it one," she said.

"Psycho-babble doesn't change facts, Jessie."

"But you like working with the horses. I've seen you." He glanced at her sharply. "I meant, I've, you know, caught a glimpse of you now and then, and you seemed to be having a good time. Not that I was watching or anything." She gave up and stared at the ground. One day before she died she promised herself she was going to learn to think before opening her mouth.

"Yes, I like working with the horses."

"Then that's something." She risked looking up at him. He didn't seem angry.

"Okay," he said. "You win. It is something. Not much, but something."

"There. I knew it would all work out." She tucked her hand under his left arm and leaned against him. They started walking toward the lodge. "There's a big antique auction in a couple of weeks. I'm going to be going there to buy most of the pieces for the furnishings. It's a high class event, so I should be able to get some really nice things." She told herself to let go of him, but she didn't want to. She liked the feel of his body close to her. She liked being reminded of how he had touched her and made her want with a frightening and unfamiliar hunger.

"Doesn't decorating rich people's homes bother you?" he asked.

"Why? It's my job and I like my work."

"But you're around all that money. You make their homes perfect, then you have to walk away from what you've done."

She shrugged. "I don't always agree with what they choose, which helps. Quite frankly, I've never fit in to society. I was raised by a single mother who worked hard to feed the two of us. Too much excess make me uncomfortable. I never know what to say to those kinds of people. They talk about things that don't interest me. Their rules are confusing. I'm not their type." She looked up at him. "But I bet you did fine."

"Oh, yeah. Navy pilots get a lot of 'A' list invitations." He sounded bitter.

They reached the steps leading up to the porch of the lodge. Jessie leaned against the railing. "Let me guess. Every woman wants you, and every man wants to tell you he could have done it too."

He raised his eyebrows. "Very good. You've figured it out."

"Not all of it," she said. "But I'm beginning to."

Eight

Jessie stepped into the lodge and immediately ducked back outside. The painters had arrived. She was probably the only decorator in the world who hated the smell of paint.

It was early yet, barely after eight in the morning. Dew still clung to the plants, and the air was misty and cool. She clutched her denim coat closer to her body and looked around. If they were painting, they would be at it for days. This would be a good time to take care of business she had in San Francisco. By the time she came back, they would be upstairs and not stinking up her work place.

She turned and headed for Mike's house. As always the sight of the building made her fingers itch for a pencil. She could turn the inside of that house into a beautiful home, all the while maintaining the charm inherent in the structure. One of these days, when Mike wasn't mad at her, and she hadn't put her foot in her mouth for over two hours, she was going to offer to draw up plans.

She went around to the back and knocked on the kitchen door. Grady answered.

"Just how I like to start my morning," he said. "Staring at a pretty face. Come on in, little lady. We were having some breakfast. Are you hungry?"

"Thanks." She slipped in past him. "Just coffee, if you have it."

"Comin' right up."

She saw Mike sitting at the table and reading the paper. When he looked up, she gave him a quick smile. He returned it and pushed out a chair with his foot.

"Have a seat."

She sat in the chair and accepted the cup of coffee. Grady took the chair opposite her.

"What brings you up here?" the older man asked.

"The painters have started in the lodge," she said, stirring in a teaspoon of sugar and some milk. "Until they move upstairs, I won't be able to get much work done. I need to go to San Francisco for some company business, so I wanted to let you know I'd be gone for a couple of days."

She risked a quick glance at Mike. He met her gaze, but his blue eyes gave nothing away. When she felt a sharp stab of disappointment, she realized that she'd hoped he might miss her.

"Have a good time," Grady said. Outside, a car pulled up next to the house. "That'll be Mrs. McGregor." He sprang from his chair and started for the door.

"He sure seems excited," Jessie said.

"She brings him fresh Danish," Mike said.

Jessie laughed. "That would make me happy to see her, too."

"Stay and have one."

"No thanks. I don't eat sweets if I can help it." She patted her thighs. "I come from a long line of Italian women who have very ample figures."

He set the paper down and leaned toward her. "Why won't you believe you're exactly right the way you are?"

His intensity drew her. She found herself clutching her coffee cup to keep from reaching out to touch him. In his red work shirt and jeans, he looked more handsome than any one man had the right to be. But it was more than just good looks that set her heart to thumping in her chest. It was his gentleness with the horses and the way he'd apologized and the touch of his hand on her body and his smile and his wounded soul.

Mike Coburn didn't look anything like Brandon, didn't walk like him, or talk like him. They'd lived very different lives. Yet there was a similarity between the two men. Mike had all of Brandon's best qualities—and that scared her to death.

Was she attracted to the man, or the memories he invoked? Was she dealing completely with the present, or was this potentially heart-breaking relationship about trying to fix the past. Was she deluding herself when she thought she and Mike might have a chance at a relationship? Was she listening to her body, or her heart? Too many questions, she thought, forcing herself to break free of Mike's gaze. Too much had happened too fast.

"Jessie." Mike covered one of her hands with his, and squeezed her gently. "I—"

The back door opened and Grady came in carrying a bakery box. "I can smell 'em. These darlings are fresh out of the oven. The box is still warm."

Mrs. McGregor trailed behind him, carrying a grocery bag in one hand and mail in the other. "You would think that man hasn't eaten in days," she said, staring fondly at Grady who was now opening the box and pulling out one of the pastries. She set the groceries on the counter and handed Mike the mail, then she headed back out.

"Let me help you," he said, rising out of his chair.

"Nonsense. I was carrying food long before you were out of diapers. Read your letters. I'm getting paid to do this." She winked at him and left the room.

"Here you go, little lady." Grady put a plate down in front of Jessie.

The bear claw was still warm; she could tell by the way the frosting hadn't hardened yet. Her stomach growled. Jessie firmly pushed the plate away. "No, thanks, I'm not hungry."

Grady put a cheese danish in front of Mike, took a second for himself and joined her. "A man likes something to hold onto in the dark," he said, winking at her. "You need to eat to keep your fine shape.

She remembered how Mike had kissed and tended to her breasts as if they were more precious and lovely than any he had previously encountered. Maybe Grady had a point. She drew in a deep breath and realized her jeans fit exactly as she wanted them to. She shook her head. "I ate breakfast, I don't need anything else. Quit fussing over me."

Grady turned to Mike for support. "You tell her. One little bear claw isn't going to hurt."

Mike didn't answer. Jessie looked up at him. He held a letter in his hand and stared at it as if it was alive. He'd paled under his tan, and his hands shook. Suddenly, he tossed the letter down, swore and pushed back from the table. He looked at both of them, started to speak, then rose and walked out without saying a word.

"What happened?" she asked.

Grady leaned across the table and picked up the envelope. He scanned the return address. "It's from that boy's mother."

"What boy?"

Grady put the envelope back down and rested his elbows on the table. His forehead furrowed as he drew his bushy eyebrows together. "You know how Mike hurt his hand?"

She thought for a minute. "He said something about some kid being in the way, but that's all."

"Tim Evans was on the same carrier as Mike. They'd been at sea less than two weeks. Tim was still puking his guts out everyday. He was on the flight deck, trying to do his job, but he didn't feel good and he wasn't paying attention. He walked too close behind a jet, right as the pilot was about to start the engine. The kid would have been fried. Mike pulled him out of the way, but in the process, he got his hand crushed. This letter—" he motioned to the piece of paper "—is from the boy's mother. She wants Mike to speak with the boy. Accept his apology for ruining his flying career."

"He won't talk to him?" she asked.

"Nope. Not since the day he threw Tim out of his hospital room."

"That's awful." Jessie understood Mike's anger, but she also felt for the young man who must carry a huge burden of guilt.

"The mother has written a couple of times before. He usually tosses out the letters."

Mrs. McGregor bustled in carrying two more bags. "Sorry to take so long. I'd brought some food for the construction workers and I had to deliver it to them. So, what do we want for lunch?"

As Grady turned to answer her, Jessie slipped out of her seat and walked outside. She could see Mike in the corral. He was working on his roping. This time he had a horse in with him and he was trying to capture it.

She walked over and stood next to the railing. She thought he might just ignore her, but he coiled the rope and approached. Although it would warm up later, it was a cool morning and his breath came out in clouds of fog. The denim jacket he wore hugged his broad shoulders and hung open in front. His Stetson hid his eyes from view, but she could feel his pain. He held the rope in his left hand, his right hung uselessly at his side.

She wished she knew if her feelings for Mike were about the present or the past. Was it because she couldn't walk away from someone wounded, or was she trying to relive her marriage and have a happy ending this time? Using Mike to make up for Brandon's death would be a horrible mistake for both of them.

She drew in a deep breath. Either way, she was trying to fix Mike, and she knew however hard she tried she would fall far short of what he needed. But she still had to try.

"You want to talk about it?" she asked, when he stopped in front of her.

"No."

She stared at the ground. This was harder than she'd thought. What if he wasn't interested? Worse, what if he was? "I'm leaving for San Francisco in a couple of hours. Want to come with me?"

He reached up and pushed his hat back far enough that she could see his eyes and the fire that flared there. "How long are you planning on staying?"

"Two or three days."

He would use her to get lost. She knew that. At least sharing her body with him would give her a sense of helping. With Brandon, there was nothing she could do for him. He had everything without her.

Mike dropped the rope to the ground and climbed through the railing. He pulled the glove off his left hand and touched her cheek. Despite the chill of the morning, he felt warm and alive. She turned her head toward his caress and knew she needed to be with him as much or more than he needed to be with her. They would get lost in each other. The risk, the price she might have to pay later, be damned.

"Where would I stay?" he asked.

"There are several lovely hotels in town," she said, then swallowed. "I have an apartment." Now came the hard part. She drew in a deep breath and looked him in the eye. "You're welcome to stay with me."

"In your bed?"

"Yes," she whispered, wanting to look away, but caught and held in his mesmerizing gaze.

"Fine," he said, and dropped a quick kiss on her mouth. "I'll drive. Meet me in the garage in an hour."

Mike down-shifted and pressed hard on the gas. The Porche sped up the hill and he easily passed the slower truck. He moved back into the right lane and glanced at Jessie.

She'd changed out of her jeans and bright sweater into a purple dress with a matching jacket. The cuffs and collar were red, and she wore dangling earrings that matched. Curvy legs stretched down to purple pumps. She wore more make-up than usual and smelled as tempting as ever.

He returned his attention to the road and grinned. He had a full day planned for them. He loved San Francisco and had spent a lot of time there. He would take her to a dynamite restaurant on the water, then dancing. He knew he was acting like a teenager, but he wanted to impress her. He remembered her beatup van, and the fact that she'd been widowed young. She probably didn't have much money for any luxuries in life. He wasn't rolling in money, but he had enough. Some came from investments from when he was in the Navy, but most of his modest fortune was the result of the inheritance that had allowed him to buy and refurbish the ranch.

He decided he was going to take care of Jessie and show her the time of her life, for these three days. And the nights— Yeah, he would make those special, too.

"This is such a pretty drive," she said. They'd cut over to the coast and were winding along the narrow road between the mountains and the ocean. "I always forget how beautiful it all is."

"Did you grow up around here?" he asked.

"No. Nearer Sacramento. I went to college in San Francisco, though. What about you?"

"I'm an Oklahoma boy. Actually, I majored in engineering up at Northwestern."

"I'm impressed. So while I was studying light and texture and cutting out dress patterns, you were using your slide rule."

He gave her a wink. "We had calculators."

She leaned back in her seat and laughed. "I'm not great at math. Neither is my mom. And my dad . . ." She shrugged. "I never knew much about him."

"I'm sorry," he said, automatically and then was surprised to find out he was sorry. He liked Jessie. She drove him crazy on a regular basis, but she was easy to be with. She let him forget.

"Do you have any kids?" she asked.

"Isn't the normal question to ask if I have a wife?"

"I didn't want to get personal."

He glanced at her. She was smiling. "Asking about kids isn't personal?"

"I knew you weren't married now because Grady had told me you two were single guys who needed a woman's touch in the lodge. So I figured if there was an ex-wife, you wouldn't want to talk about her."

"I don't follow your logic, but I believe you meant well. No kids. What about you?"

He happened to glance at her as he asked, and saw the flash of pain on her face. She turned and looked out the window, toward the mountains. "None. Brandon and I wanted them, but he said we should wait. Then he was gone."

"How'd you two meet?" he asked.

"Through work. He lived and breathed Ross Building and Design." She shifted in her seat. "He loved building things, but the truth is, he was a horrible construction worker. It took him hours to put together a set of bookcases for his study, and even then, they came out crooked." She chuckled. He liked the soft sound. "He could read a blue-print and plan a building. But he was a menace at a construction site."

"Sounds like you still miss him."

"Sometimes," she admitted. "But he was gone so much. I loved him terribly, but I was never enough." She glanced at him. "The ultimate female fantasy, to be all things to one man."

"I thought the ultimate female fantasy was shopping with an unlimited budget."

She leaned over and gently slugged him in the arm. "Don't be a chauvinist. Not all women like to shop."

"Do you?"

She looked down at her dress. "I have my moments. Brandon

hated me to wear bright colors. I think they embarrassed him. After he'd been gone almost a year, I threw out all my dark things and bought clothes that I liked." She grimaced. "Then the bills came."

He realized that in her own way, Jessie had been lonely, too. For a moment, he wanted to pull her close and promise to keep her safe from the world. He wanted to tell her that he would take care of her financially and make her fears go away. The desire to protect her was unfamiliar, but he liked it. He felt whole around her—he felt like a man.

"I happen to like your bright colors," he said. "I hope you brought something dressy. I think we should try to catch a show while we're in town."

"Really? Oh, Mike, that would be great. I love the theater." She leaned over and rested her head on his shoulder. "Thank you for being so nice."

She was soft and feminine. He wanted to pull over and take her right here in the car. He glanced at the small interior of the Porche. On second thought, he could wait until they were at her place. He flexed his right hand, then tightened it into a fist. His range of motion was slightly better. He still couldn't write worth beans, and buttons drove him crazy, but the part that mattered still worked. He would please Jessie tonight.

As they drove into the city, she gave him directions to Ross Construction. "My meeting will take about two hours," she said, taking a key out of her purse. "You want to go get settled at the apartment? I can just grab a cab back. It's only about fifteen minutes away."

"Sure," he said, liking the way she blushed when she handed him the key. Maybe he should change his plans around. Maybe they should make love first.

He rounded the corner and stopped in front of the tall building bearing the name and logo of the construction company. She opened the door to step out, then looked back at him.

"Thanks for coming with me." Her brown eyes darkened with delight and desire. She leaned forward.

Low in his belly, anticipation coiled. It had been too long since he'd wanted a woman. Funny how this time, the ache was specific for Jessie. Thoughts of her naked filled his mind.

He kissed her briefly. Their eyes met. She reached up and brushed his mouth with her thumb.

"Hmm, you don't really look great in my lipstick," she said, then laughed.

He grinned in return.

Behind her, one of the glass doors opened, and a man rushed toward the car. "Mrs. Ross," he called. "Hello. The board is all assembled."

Jessie looked at the man in his tailored suit and expensive shoes. "Thank you, Jeffery. I'll be right there."

"Mrs. Ross?" Mike said, confused.

Jessie shrugged. "My other life. I hide from it as much as possible."

No, he thought in growing disbelief. It wasn't possible. His stomach knotted as he looked at the logo on the side of the building. Ross Building and Design. "Mrs. Ross?" he practically shouted.

Jessie bit her lower lip. "What's the matter?"

"You're supposed to be Jessie Layton."

"I am Jessie Layton. At least that's the name I use for work. Brandon's name carried so much baggage that after he died I went back to my maiden name." She stared at him, obviously confused. "I thought you knew. Grady and I had a long talk about it."

"Grady didn't see fit to tell me."

It was more than anger, he realized, as the emotions tumbled through him. Pain and humiliation flooded his being. Jessie Ross.

"Let me guess," he said bitterly. "You own the company."

"Not all of it. About forty percent."

"Bitch."

She jumped as if he'd hit her. "Mike, what's going on? Why are you acting like this?"

"You lied to me."

"I didn't. I thought you knew."

He didn't want to hear her explanations. He thought about his plans for their time in the city. He was going to be a big shot, show her the town. Dazzle her with a couple of expensive dinners and tickets to a show. He swore. He was going to be a man for her. He shook his head. She could buy and sell him about a hundred times over. She'd played him for a fool.

"Get out," he said, staring straight ahead.

"Mike, I want to explain."

"Explain what?" He turned toward her. He saw the concern in

her eyes, and the fear, but he didn't give a damn. "That you're some rich widow? What the hell are you doing on my ranch?"

"I love my work. After Brandon died, it was all I had."

"Sure, lady. What does that make me? Your pet project? Is this be kind to cripples week?"

She flinched as if each word was a physical blow. Tears formed in her eyes, then spilled onto her cheek.

"Get out of my car."

"Mike—"

He shifted into gear. She grabbed her purse and stepped onto the sidewalk. Barely pausing to jerk her door shut, he pulled into traffic and sped down the road.

Nine

Jessie opened the door to the penthouse apartment and stepped into the cool, tiled foyer. Her luggage stood beside the marble table, her key had been tossed into a glass dish. The doorman had already told her Mike had come and gone over two hours ago, but she'd hoped he would at least have left her a note.

She looked around the elegant living room, then walked into the kitchen. Nothing. No dust, no sound, no note. She kicked off her pumps in the long hallway and continued moving toward her bedroom. She'd redone most of the apartment about six months after Brandon had died, so she was able to walk into the giant room with its over-sized sleigh bed and floor-to-ceiling windows without remembering him. But the muted wallpaper and soothing colors of the bedspread and carpet didn't lift her spirits at all. Instead of Brandon, she pictured Mike as she had for most of the trip up to the city. She imagined him lying naked in her bed, smiling at her, wanting her. She thought about them making love, healing each other with touches and murmured words of need. She thought of all the things they would do for each other, be with each other. A fantasy, she told herself when the tears threatened again. Nothing else.

She walked over to the window and stared out at the city. It was late afternoon and the fog had long since burned away. She could see the bay and traffic already snarling on the Golden Gate bridge.

Where was he now? Would he call her? And why had he thought she'd lied to him.

"I swear I thought you knew," she whispered to the silent room. "I would never have lied."

Would he believe her? She shook her head. Of course not. As wounded as he was, Mike managed to carry a pretty big chip on his shoulder.

She moved to the bed and sat down. Her fingers rubbed against the spread, feeling the contrast of Belgian lace over satin. Why did it matter? So he hadn't known that she was Brandon's widow and that she owned a large percentage of the company. How did that change anything between them? She had a seat on the board because she was required to, but aside from that, she had nothing to do with the day-to-day operations. She had her choice of decorating assignments and only took the ones that interested her. She'd decided to take on the dude ranch, a small job for her, because she'd liked the location and Grady had charmed the socks off of her when they'd talked on the phone.

She blinked back her tears and told herself to forget Mike. She would send someone else to finish the work at the ranch. She would take a vacation. Maybe a cruise, or a couple of weeks in London. The place didn't matter as long as she was far away from Mike Coburn.

She got up and walked over to her closet. After changing into jeans and a sweater, she sat on the floor and pulled on an old pair of red cowboy boots. As she rubbed the scuffed leather, she remembered how Brandon had cringed when she bought them. He preferred her in muted colors and classical styles. He hadn't liked her sensual side, not even in bed. Jessie leaned against the closet wall. Mike had seem to revel in her body, loving her breasts and kissing her until she'd thought she might die from the pleasure. Mike had—

"Stop it," she commanded herself. She had to forget about him. She had to stop thinking about him because there was nothing she could do about him or the situation. In his own way, Mike was exactly like Brandon. He didn't like parts of her, either. He didn't like that she was rich.

She went into the kitchen and thought about fixing some dinner. The housekeeper still came three days a week, although there wasn't anything for her to do. She regularly stocked the fridge. Jessie stared at the food, then turned away. She wasn't hungry. No matter how she tried to dismiss Mike from her mind, she couldn't forget the look of betrayal on his face, and the pain in his eyes when he'd figured out who she really was.

She knew he'd spent the last six months trying to pretend he was dead. Then she came along and forced him to admit he was alive. Now she had hurt him in his most vulnerable place. She didn't understand why he was so upset, but she was smart enough to figure out it had to do with the money, with her having a lot more than he did.

"Doesn't he know that doesn't matter?" she asked out loud. "Are all men this stupid?"

The last question made her smile. She walked back to the foyer and stared at her suitcase. She knew he wouldn't call her or come back to her. He was an injured warrior, and she'd just dealt the death blow. He would retreat to a safe place and wait to die. She had to let him go. But she couldn't.

She opened the top drawer of the marble table and pulled out the set of keys there. Then she picked up her suitcase and walked out of her apartment.

In the underground parking lot, she opened the trunk of her midnight-blue Mercedes and tossed her bag inside. Then she got behind the wheel and started the engine. She took the van on working trips because it could hold all her supplies, but it was a company vehicle. This one was hers. A gift from Brandon, for her thirtieth birthday. She remembered she'd asked for a weekend away. Anywhere, she'd told him. As long as it was just the two of them. Instead he'd taken her to dinner, given her the keys to this car and, shortly after they'd returned to the apartment, kissed her on the forehead and told her he had to work.

She'd been so angry, she'd moved out of their bedroom. He'd never understood why she'd been upset. He'd even promised to spend more time with her, when his busy season was over. She hadn't returned to his bedroom. She'd been waiting for him to ask her to, but he never had. Two months later, he died.

She told herself she could have tried harder with Brandon, but she knew it wasn't true. He'd made his choices long before he'd ever met her. But with Mike . . .

She leaned her head on the steering wheel. Oh, please Lord, let her not be making another mistake. She straightened up, put the car in reverse, and backed out of the space. When she reached the exit to the street, she put on her signal and turned toward the road heading back to the ranch.

It was almost nine at night when she reached the small town twenty miles from the ranch. Some instinct made her slow as she neared the bar Mike had run to the last time she'd upset him. Sure enough, a shiny black Porche sat in front of the wooden building. She pulled her car next to it and stopped. What was she going to say to him? It wasn't hard to figure he wasn't going to be all that pleased to see her. But they couldn't just leave it hanging between them. Not after the things he'd accused her of.

Drawing in a deep breath for courage, she got out and locked her car. As she neared the bar, she saw a couple of men walk out of the building and glance at her. Their gazes slipped past her to the two expensive cars sitting side by side on the dirt parking lot. One of them nudged the other and they both gave a low whistle.

"Leave it to me to blend in completely," Jessie muttered, as she pushed open the door and entered the bar.

It wasn't as late as the last time she'd been here, and there were more people milling about in the room. Several couples danced on a makeshift floor off to one side. Booths lined both walls, and tables sat in front of the bar itself.

Jessie looked around and spotted a familiar pair of broad shoulders in a white dress shirt. Mike sat in a booth at the end of the room. His hat was on the table in front of him, and he was bent over a glass.

She paused just behind him, gathering the courage to approach and trying to figure out what on earth she was supposed to say.

"Mike?" Not the most original line, but the best she could come up with under pressure.

He didn't turn around. He raised the glass to his mouth and drank. He was drinking beer. He drained the liquid, slammed the glass down, tossed a ten on the table and slid out of the booth. When he turned toward her, she looked up at him, prepared to smile or say something, but his shuttered expression silenced her. It was as if he'd built a wall around himself and no one was going to get through.

Certainly not her. He grabbed his hat and set it on his head, then walked past her as if she didn't exist.

He was almost at the door before she got herself together enough to go after him. She shouldered her way through the ever-thickening crowd.

"Mike, wait."

He didn't slow. He pushed open the front door and stepped out into the night. She ran across the bar room and followed him outside.

"I know you're angry at me. I don't understand why, but can't we talk about it? If nothing else, you shouldn't be driving after drinking."

He'd already opened the door to the Porche. However, at her last statement, he slammed it shut and walked over to her. She stood on the bottom step, so they were almost at eye-level.

"Not that it's any of your damn business," he said, his voice a low growl, "but I have had exactly one light beer over the last three hours. You seem to have this need to do good deeds, so I'm sure you'll sleep better knowing I'm not going to crash on the way back to the ranch."

Anger radiated out from him, and beneath that, primal rage threatened. He frightened her. She knew she was the cause of his suffering, but she didn't understand why. When he turned to leave, she grabbed his sleeve.

"Wait."

He jerked his arm free. "If you know what's good for you, stay the hell away from me."

The music from the juke box filtered out into the night. It was cooler here in the mountains than it had been in the city and she clutched her coat close to her body. Mike still wore the jeans and white shirt he'd put on that morning, but he didn't seem to notice the cold.

"I'm sorry you think I did something wrong," she said.

"I *think* you did something wrong? No, lady. I *know* it. What the hell kind of game were you playing? Did you get off on making me look like a complete jerk?"

The helpless feeling returned. She brushed her hair out of her face and stared at him. The man she'd imagined loving had disappeared in the cold countenance of an angry stranger. "I never purposely hid my position from you. Grady knew; I thought he told you. I wasn't trying to make a fool of you. I was trying . . ."

"You're damn good," he said," and she knew it wasn't a compliment. "You really had me going there. I never saw it coming."

A truck drove up. He grabbed her arm and pulled her away from the entrance to the bar. They stood close together in the shadows, a couple of feet from the front of her car.

"You played me for a fool, lady," he said, not letting go of her.

Jessie suspected he didn't even know he was holding on to her. She didn't try to escape. "You're wrong, Mike. I tried to be a friend."

"Most of my friends manage to keep their clothes on."

She gasped, knowing he referred to that afternoon in the barn. "How dare you," she said, her own temper beginning to burn. "How dare you try and cheapen that moment? It was special to me, and you can tell me anything you like, but I know in my heart it was special to you, too."

He bent down until his face was inches from hers. "In the rodeo they call the women who pick up the cowboys 'buckle bunnies.' Pilots aren't that polite. But that's all it was, wasn't it? A mercy lay." He reached for his jeans. "Fine, babe, it's dark here. Let's see what you've got. I'll make sure you like it. Then you can have it both ways. You can enjoy the sex and earn your reward in heaven for screwing the cripple."

He'd opened the top button on his fly and was reaching for the second when she reached out and slapped him. His head jerked up and he glared at her. The parking lot lights made his eyes glow as if lit with an unholy light. He touched the darkening spot on his cheek.

"If I could hit hard enough, I'd beat you up," she said. She leaned close to him and planted her hands on her hips. "I'm not afraid of you, Mike Coburn. I'm not afraid of anyone. You can stomp and scream and accuse all you want, but I'm not the one you're angry with. But I'm an easy target, so go ahead. Take out your bitterness on me. I guess I've taken Grady's place."

He looked startled and took a step back. She moved closer. He wasn't getting off that easy. "Do you want me to apologize for not being a poor widow? Should I be *sorry* I married well and that my husband left me his shares in the company? Would that make you happy?"

"You don't understand."

"You bet I don't." She drew in a deep breath. "Here's a news flash for you Mike. We all know why you can't fly. Your hand doesn't work right. You can hide it all you want, but the truth exists. You think it would have been better to die like some stupid hero. That would have been the easy way. Well, you didn't die. And you should be damn grateful you're still here, taking up room with your pitiful hide. You're supposed to be a warrior? Act like one buddy. Grow up. We've all got problems."

He glared down at her like he wanted to wrap his arms around her neck and strangle her. "What problems do you have?"

"You, for one. Your hand isn't working a hundred percent. So what? You can't fly. So what? You can do other things. You're still a capable person."

Mike started to walk away. He stopped and spun to face her. Now he was in the shadows and she couldn't see the expression on his face. She wondered if he'd done that on purpose. "If I'm so capable, why did the Navy cut me loose, and why didn't Pam even wait until I was out of the hospital before dumping me?"

He waited, but she had nothing to say. Pam? Who was Pam? She'd never heard the name before, but she knew hearing it now wasn't good news. A woman had left him because of his injury. She opened her mouth to speak but no words came out.

Mike laughed harshly. "Amazing. I managed to shut you up at last." With that, he headed for his car and got inside. She was still standing in the parking lot when he drove off into the night.

Ten

"I didn't expect to see you here," Grady said from the front door of her trailer. "Can I come in?"

"Sure." Jessie pushed aside the sketch she'd been making and walked over to the kitchen area of the trailer. "Want some coffee?"

"Sounds good." He took the cup she offered, then looked around the compact living space. "Nice," he commented. "I like what you've done with the plants."

He took a seat on one of the two couches, and she sat opposite him. It was midmorning, but she felt tired and achy. She hadn't slept at all last night. She alternated between staring at the ceiling and pacing the length of the trailer. The situation with Mike had gotten way out of hand. The way she saw it, the only solution was a timely retreat.

She twisted her hands together and stared at her nails. Because of her drawing, she'd never been able to grow them long, or bothered with painting them. She'd always wanted elegant nails. She'd always wanted a lot of things.

Grady sat silently in front of her, sipping his coffee and looking around the trailer. He was waiting for her to say something. Or collecting his thoughts before firing her. She might as well save him the trouble.

"I've almost finished the sketches on the cabins," she said. "I'll be done late this afternoon. I've put a call into the office and as soon as I get the name of my replacement, I'll let you know. I'm sure you'll be pleased with whomever they pick." She rushed through her statement, then glanced up at him.

He'd rested one ankle on his opposite knee and leaned back into the cushions. There was a planter with bright geraniums right behind his head and his red hair clashed with the color of the blooms.

He raised his bushy eyebrows and took a sip of coffee. "Never took you to be the type who'd run away."

The jab scored a direct hit. She straightened in her seat. "I'm not running. It's obvious that Mike and I are destined to make each other miserable. All I do is hurt him, and stick my foot in my mouth. It would be better for both of us if I left."

"Oh, I don't know about that."

"How can you say that? Do you know what happened yesterday?"

"No." He leaned to his left and set the cup down. "I do know you and Mike were supposed to be gone for three days, and he came home late last night—alone. Feel free to fill in the details."

She looked back at her hands. "I can't." It would be too much of a betrayal. She couldn't explain how she'd hurt Mike, the things they'd said to each other, not even to his best friend.

"You ever a cheerleader in high school?"

"What?" She glanced up at him and allowed herself a small smile. "No. I was a little too nerdy for the pep squad."

"Too bad. You might be able to understand it better then."

"Understand what."

"About being a fighter pilot."

She shook her head. "Oh, that. I know, Grady. There's this huge mystique about the whole thing. The pilots are worshipped. They risk death. They bond. But, really, it's *just* a job, isn't it?"

"Is it, little lady? Are you sure you know what you're talking about?"

She leaned forward and rested her elbows on her knees. "Okay, then you tell me. Help me understand." Maybe if she got it, she would be able to figure Mike out.

"When there's a night landing during a storm, the pilots know the deck is going to be bouncing around like a cork in a bathtub. The ship is moving forward, but the runway is at a ten degree angle. The pilot may or may not have enough fuel left to make several passes, depending on conditions, weight of the plane, that sort of thing. A plane that comes in for the landing, but doesn't hook the cable is called a bolter. You bolt one too many times you end up in the sea."

Jessie shifted until she was sitting on her leg. She propped her elbow up on the couch back. "What does this have to do with anything?"

"You end up in the sea, you've lost over a million dollars worth of equipment. And you may die."

"Mike told me this. About it being digital. You either make it or you don't."

"Did you think about what that means? When was the last time you left for work not knowing if you were going to come home alive? When was the last time your boss told you not to mess up and die?"

"I—"

He wasn't finished. Grady stared at her and frowned. "I went in a bar with Mike once. We were on leave, and went up to Boston. In less than fifteen minutes, six women had approached him, trying to make it with him. He got more medals than most, he was on the fast track to promotion. Power, glory, respect of men—"

"Adoration of women. I know all this. It doesn't explain or excuse the way he's retreated from life."

"That's because you're not understanding me, Jessie."

It was the use of her name that got her attention. For the first time since she'd arrived on the ranch, he wasn't calling her "little lady."

"Then explain it better," she said.

He looked frustrated for a moment, then smiled. "What was your least favorite subject in school?"

"Math," she answered without hesitation.

"Do you use it now?"

"Only some basic elements, for measuring, figuring out the amount of wallpaper or carpet, that sort of thing."

He reached for his coffee and took another sip. "Okay. Imagine if you went to bed tonight, and when you woke up in the morning, everything in the world was based on math."

She frowned. "What does that have to do with anything?"

"Wouldn't you be happy?"

"No, but—"

"Would it be easy for you to get along?"

She wasn't sure where he was going with this, but she was willing to trust him. "No."

"Pilots don't spend a lot of time involved in introspection. They do their job. They live hard and fast, because any day, any flight, could be their last. They don't think about the danger, or the fear because if they do, they'll lose their edge. They are the best and the brightest our country has. They are the sacrificial offering, guaranteeing our safety. That was Mike's world. But he doesn't fit there any more. Now he's in your world, where people expect him to be like you or me. He's supposed to know himself and be a regular guy. He's being forced to ask questions no one should have to ask. He doesn't have any answers. He can only do what he does best, and that is to ignore his feelings and get the job done. The only problem is he doesn't have that job anymore."

"You make it sound as if he's a different species."

"Maybe he is. If you woke up in a world filled with math, wouldn't you do anything to get things back to the way they were?"

"But Mike is more than a fighter pilot."

"You believe that, but can he? If in his eyes, he is only a fighter pilot, what does that make him now?"

"A man isn't just defined by his career."

He rose to his feet and looked down at her. "Not everyone would agree with you, little lady. Mike doesn't."

With that, he left, leaving her alone with the morning and her thoughts. She walked over to the drafting table and stared down at her sketches. What would it be like if she couldn't draw? She fingered the wool sweater she'd pulled on. The colors were bright, all blues and teals, mixed with fuchsia. She glanced around the room, at the patterned fabric and the green plants and the painted denim jacket slung over one kitchen chair.

Grady had it wrong. She would survive in a world filled with math. She would hate it, but she would survive. But if her world suddenly became black and white, that would be very different. She would fade away without her colors. A drab gray would kill her slowly, but it would kill her in the end.

Is that what was happening to Mike? Was he dying in pieces, day by day, living a hellish existence? Was it too late, or could he be saved? Could she save him, or did he have to do it all himself?

She sat down in front of the drafting table and picked up a pencil. It would be so easy to walk away. She'd already made the plans. He wouldn't miss her; no doubt he would be grateful that she was gone.

But what about everything Grady said? If the old man was right, Mike needed her support. And everything that had happened last night told her that Grady had been right. It would be cowardly and selfish to walk away.

She shook her head. Maybe not. After all, she was probably the worst person to be offering Mike any sort of help. Look how badly she'd failed with Brandon. She couldn't even keep him from working himself to death. She hadn't been enough for Brandon and she wouldn't be enough for Mike. Walking away was the only solution to both their problems. He would find someone else to help him through this. She was a fool to think she had any special skills that he needed. It would be best for both of them if she was gone.

"Whoa, boy," Mike said, reining the black gelding to a stop. "Good boy." He bent down and patted the animal's neck. After dismounting, he led the animal over to the stable and took off the saddle. When he was done, he slipped a halter over his head and took him back in the corral. He let him loose and picked up the rope he'd left hanging over a fence post.

He and the gelding had been playing this game for almost a week now. After riding the horse, he would try to rope him. It gave him roping practice and helped develop the animal's natural playful nature. He was going to be a good mount for intermediate riders at the ranch.

He raised his left hand and tossed the rope. The gelding waited then ducked away at the last minute and the rope fell harmlessly to the ground. As Mike bent over to pick it up, he inhaled a familiar scent drifting to him on the morning breeze. He didn't have to turn around to know Jessie was close by. It had been wishful thinking for him to hope he could avoid her for long. The ranch wasn't that big.

He fought the urge to disappear into the barn. He had to face her sooner or later. He'd already made an ass of himself in front of her—he'd be damned if he'd run away like a coward on top of that.

Besides, it was his own fault for believing. In those few short hours they'd driven north to the city, he'd imagined himself to be a man again, capable of pleasing a woman. He'd let himself think he was more, that he was whole.

Jessica Ross. Who had he been kidding? In that second when he'd realized who she really was, the magnitude of what he'd lost had slammed into him. The pain in his chest grew until it hurt to breathe. The hell of it was, he didn't know how to make it go away.

Without even turning around, he could tell she was close. He heard the scraping of her boot on the railing as she climbed onto the split-rail fence and sat down. He coiled his rope, but before he could throw it again, the gelding came up and nuzzled his shoulder.

"He sure has calmed down," she said, from her seat behind him.

"Yeah."

Mike shooed him away and tossed the rope. It landed cleanly over the gelding's neck.

"You're roping much better."

He didn't answer. He didn't want to talk about his hand, even though he realized she was right last night: everyone did know what was wrong with him. He wasn't fooling anyone by hiding the scars.

He threw several more times. When it became obvious Jessie wasn't going away, he walked over to where she sat on the fence. The sun was behind him and he could see her face clearly. She'd acquired a slight tan in the last few days. Her thick shoulder-length hair blew in the breeze and her breasts filled out her knit sweater. He clenched the rope to keep from touching her.

"What do you want?" he asked, when their eyes met. She looked scared and sad at the same time.

"To say I'm sorry."

He started to turn away.

"No, wait, Mike."

He paused.

"Can you spare me a minute?" she asked. "I'd like to tell you something."

Instead of answering, he leaned against the fence and folded his arms over his chest.

"I didn't know Brandon when I went to work for him," she said. "I was just a lowly assistant decorator. You remember when I told you that story about the rich lady who wanted carpet the color of her dog's accidents?"

He nodded, and wondered why she was telling him this.

"When she ordered me off the job, Brandon called me up to his office. I think he was going to fire me. I explained what had happened, and we got to talking, and he asked me to do some decorating for him. By the time the job was done, we were engaged."

Mike wanted to walk away. He didn't need to hear this story, and he didn't care about how she'd come into her money. But he refused to let her know she got to him, so he watched the gelding trot around the corral and tried not to listen to her soft voice, or acknowledge the spicy scent of her perfume.

"He was much older than I was. Attractive, powerful, wealthy. None of that really mattered to me. Before we were married, he used to take time to be with me. We would do things together. He made me feel special." She sounded as wistful as a child gazing at a puppy in a pet store window.

He glanced up at her. She was staring past him, toward the mountains. Her profile was as beautiful as the rest of her. The straight line of her small nose, the fullness of her lips, the stubborn tilt of her chin.

"All his friends said I married him for the money. My friends told me I had turned into a snob. Brandon returned to his first love—his business, and I got lost in the shuffle. I tried to make the marriage work. I tried to be enough. But I wasn't. He didn't like the way I dressed. He didn't want to have children right away." She blinked several times and looked down at him. "So after he died, it seemed easier to become plain old Jessie Layton again. Not because I was trying to hide who I was, but because it had hurt too much to be married to Brandon."

He didn't want to think about what she was telling him, but he couldn't turn away from the pleading in her eyes. "You should have told me," he said gruffly.

"I thought you knew. I swear, Mike. I would never have kept that from you. I had no reason to."

"Why are you telling me this now?"

She swallowed. "Because of last night."

He did turn away then. He walked across the corral and opened the gate. After latching it behind him, he headed for the barn. He didn't want to think about last night or the things she'd said to him. He didn't want to remember any of it.

When he reached the barn, he tossed the rope inside and headed for the house. Jessie caught up with him on the narrow path. The construction workers were all in the main building, or the private cottages. Despite the sound of hammering and power tools, they were virtually alone.

"Mike, wait." She touched his shoulder.

He shrugged off her touch and kept walking.

"I'm sorry," she said, from somewhere behind. "I never meant to hurt you."

He stopped suddenly, as if he'd run into a brick wall. Hurt him? She couldn't hurt him because he refused to feel anything. It wasn't possible for anyone to hurt him.

He spun on his heel. "Lady, you insulted me. There's a difference."

"I apologize. For what I said. For slapping you." She shrugged. "All of it."

He reached up and touched his cheek. He could still feel the sting and hear the sound of her well-timed blow. He shoved his hands into his jeans pockets, then pulled them out. "No, Jessie. Don't apologize for that. I was way out of line."

They were standing about ten feet apart. She took a step closer to him. Sunlight filtered through the trees and dappled her face as she passed from shadows to light.

"I wish I knew what was wrong," she said, holding her hands out in front of her. "I've had trouble with clients before, but nothing like this."

He allowed himself a small smile. "We do seem to bring out the worst in each other." And the best as well, he thought, remembering how she'd had the courage to bare herself to him that day in the barn. She wasn't the type of woman who gave herself easily to a man. The story about her husband proved that. She had risked his rejection or ridicule, yet she had done it for him. Last night he'd thrown it in her face.

Pain twisted in his gut. He'd never meant to become a complete bastard. He hadn't wanted the bitterness to spill out and destroy others. His own destruction should have been enough.

"I'm sorry, too," he said, when she stopped directly in front of him. He reached out and touched her soft cheek. "I know in my gut you didn't lie to me yesterday. I was surprised by the information, and I reacted."

"I know."

She smiled. Her skin moved under his fingertips, and he wanted to pull her close and kiss her until she remembered nothing about yesterday and what he'd said, until all that existed was their mutual pleasure. But he couldn't do that. Not now, not ever.

"Does this mean you're not going to fire me?" she asked.

He lowered his hand to his side. "Do you still *want* to work here?"

"Yes. As long as we can be friends."

Friends. That was a new one. He'd never been friends with a woman before. "I'm not sure I'm up to it."

"Give it a try," she said. "You might surprise yourself."

"Okay. Friends."

"Good." Her smile widened and she held out her right hand. "Let's shake on it."

He wanted to run again, but he couldn't. Not now. Her smile got a little shaky around the edges, but it didn't fade. She hadn't put her foot in her mouth; she was doing this on purpose.

He stared at her hand. She wore her nails short. No rings, no polish. It was just a woman's hand. Nothing to be frightened of. All he had to do was place his next to hers. Palm to palm, fingers to wrist.

He couldn't. He might hurt her. Or worse, he might make a fool of himself. What if she—

What if she what? he asked himself. As Jessie had pointed out last night, she already knew about his injury.

He clenched his teeth and looked into her eyes. She waited patiently, her arm extended. Her expression pleaded with him, and suddenly he could deny her nothing.

He reached out his arm and took her hand in his. Concentrating hard, he tightened his unresponsive muscles. His fingers moved slightly. He could almost feel the warmth of her skin next to his. He pumped his arm once and released her. The smile she gave him was dazzling enough to block out the sun.

He smiled back.

She looked away suddenly, as if confused. She ducked her head, mumbled something about having to get some work done, and took off down the path. He stared after her until she disappeared around a tree, then he turned and headed for the house.

When he reached the porch he paused and looked out over the ranch. Several horses played in the outer corrals. He could hear birds calling to each other and the sound of construction in the building. The smell of paint and fresh cut wood drifted to him. He inhaled deeply. It was all coming together. It wasn't the deck of a carrier, but maybe it wasn't exactly a prison either.

In the distance, he saw Jessie heading for the lodge. She'd tucked her sketch pad under one arm. There was a backpack slung over her shoulder and she walked with an easy grace.

They were friends. They'd sealed the bargain with a handshake. He slowly closed his bad hand into a fist. It didn't hurt too much. As Jessie moved out of his field of vision he knew if he'd still been flying jets, he would never have taken the time to get to know her. He would have given her the onceover and passed her up in favor of some leggy blonde. He would never have known what it was like to care about her.

The thought caught him off guard. But it was true. He cared about her. He liked her. He squinted against the sunlight and turned toward the house. He hadn't thought he would ever feel anything but pain and disappointment.

As he reached for the door, he told himself liking or not liking didn't matter. He had no room for Jessie in his life, and there was no place for him in hers. She was a rich widow and the majority stockholder in a major corporation. He was a broken-down pilot with a fledgling dude ranch. He looked at his scarred hand, then shoved it in his pocket.

When he came right down to it, he didn't have one damn thing to offer her.

Eleven

"But I like this one," Mrs. McGregor said, pointing at the white molding.

"Woman, are you daft?" Grady asked. "It makes the room look fussy."

Mrs. McGregor pulled herself up to her full height, which was about three or four inches taller than Grady's, and stared down at the man. "You may not call me *daft*."

Jessie watched as he took one look at the fire in her eyes, and started to back down. "Now, don't get into a tizzy, little lady."

"Tizzy? Little lady?" Mrs. McGregor glanced over at Jessie who was struggling to keep a straight face. "If this is the sort of talk you have to put up with in your profession, I don't know how you stand it." With that she turned and marched off, nearly running into Mike as he tried to enter the soon-to-be library.

"Oh, fine," Grady said, walking after her. "Blame your bad taste on me. I'm not the one who wants to turn a perfectly good library into a bordello."

When they were safely out of earshot, Jessie gave in and sank to the floor laughing.

"What's going on?" Mike asked, staring first at her, then at the retreating couple. "I thought we were supposed to discuss molding."

"Grady and Mrs. McGregor were having a heated discussion about the whole thing." She gasped for breath and wiped her eyes. "She likes the molding. He thinks it looks—"

"Like a bordello, yeah I heard." Mike shoved his hands into his pockets and studied the strips of wood she'd tacked up on the wall. "I'm kind of in the middle. What do you think?"

"Oh, no. I'm staying out of it."

Grady stomped back into the room. "Fool woman," he muttered. He marched over to where Jessie was sitting on the floor. "I vote for no molding."

She raised her hands in a gesture of surrender. "Fine with me. I didn't know everyone would be so touchy about this."

Mike peered at the strips on the wall. "I don't know Grady. I kind of like this one," he said, pointing.

The older man glared at him and mumbled something about "Stupid officers," and "Official incompetence."

Jessie pulled her knees to her chest and watched the two men together. They argued good-naturedly, their affection for each other creating a tangible bond. For a foolish minute, she allowed herself to wonder what it would be like to live in a place like this, surrounded by family and friends. Her life had always been so solitary. First it had been just her and her mother. Then she'd been alone. She'd lived with Brandon, but he'd been gone so much, it had been like being on her own. Now she was a widow. She'd spent a lot of her life lonely, she thought, wondering how that had come to be.

Mike would be surprised if she told him, but she envied him his household. When the ranch got going, this place would be a madhouse. A tiny pain stabbed her chest. She recognized it as envy. When this job was over, she didn't want to move on. It wasn't just about Mike, although there was something deep inside of him that called to her. It was also about the ranch, Grady, and Mrs. McGregor. It was the mountains and the main house that she would love to decorate.

She watched him argue playfully with his friend. Morning sun streamed through the tall, narrow windows between the floor-to-ceiling bookcases. The light caught his blond hair and made it gleam. With his broad shoulders and lean, muscled body, he looked fit enough to wrestle a bear. If not for the scars on his hand, no one would know he'd ever been injured.

It wasn't just his good looks that made her heart flutter in her chest. It was his humor and the way he worked so hard to hide his weakness. It was his gentleness with the horses and his pride. It was his pain and the way he made her feel when he touched her. It was his desperate need to hope, even when he constantly told himself there was nothing left to hope for. It was the way she looked forward to seeing him and being with him.

Oh, that was a dangerous line of thought, she told herself. She scrambled to her knees and collected her notebook containing the lists of furniture she would need. As she rose to her feet, Mike glanced over at her.

"Where are you going?" he asked.

"There's an auction about forty miles from here," she said, then looked at her watch. "It starts in a couple of hours. I thought I'd go check it out."

"You want some company?" he asked.

She told herself it was foolish to be pleased at his question, that if she didn't watch herself, she would be heading for heartbreak, but she couldn't deny the truth. She *wanted* to be with him. "I'd like that."

"What about the molding?" Grady asked, still bristling.

Mike winked at Jessie. "I like it," he said, and ducked out of the room. Laughing, Jessie followed, leaving Grady to argue with himself.

As they drove off, Jessie tried not to think about the last time she and Mike had been away together. That trip had ended in disaster. This was different, she told herself, as she rolled down the truck's passenger window. They were just going to spend the afternoon together. No sex; no pressure.

"Not much longer until the ranch opens," she said.

"Tell me about it. Four weeks. Grady's done most of the hiring, but there are still a few jobs to be filled. We've got some college kids coming at the end of the week. They'll help out in the stables and at the lodge. I just hope the cottages are done on time. We're already filling up with reservations."

She grinned.

He glanced at her. "What's so funny?"

"You sound like an experienced hotelier, complaining about reservations and staff."

He gripped the steering wheel with his left hand and shrugged. "Maybe it's not as horrible as I'd thought," he admitted. "Don't you dare say 'I told you so' or you'll be walking back to the ranch."

"Me?" She touched her chest. "I'm sure I don't know what you're talking about. Why would I say anything like that? Just because I had to point out how beautiful the ranch is and how much you must have liked it at one time to have bought it in the first place, and the fact that—"

"Jessie," he growled playfully, cutting her off.

"I would never say a word."

He balled his right hand up into a loose fist and gently cuffed her arm. "Troublemaker."

"Always," she promised. When he dropped his hand to his lap, she studied the fine network of scars along his fingers and across the back of his hand. When she'd first arrived, he could barely make a fist. Now the motion seemed almost effortless. She wanted to touch his scars and ease whatever pain he still felt. Did he have any feeling in his hand? She knew it was difficult for him to manipulate his fingers, but she didn't know if it was because his fingers were numb or just unresponsive.

She raised her gaze to his chest. He wore a cream-colored shirt tucked into regulation blue jeans. As always, his handsome face made her catch her breath.

"What are you staring at?" he asked, never taking his gaze from the road.

"You," she answered without thinking. "You're so damn good-looking."

The silence in the cab made her realize she'd spoken her thoughts aloud. She covered her mouth with her hand and prayed he would just let the comment go by. God was not on her side.

"Not just good-looking, but 'damn' good-looking?" he asked, his voice teasing.

"I refuse to discuss this," she said, staring out the window.

"You're not half-bad yourself."

"Oh, thank you for that generous compliment."

"Any time." He chuckled.

She grinned in return. She loved to hear him laugh. She wished she could hold onto the sound forever. In a way, she wished she'd known Mike before the accident, back when he was whole. Not because she cared that his hand didn't work, but because she suspected his arrogance would have delighted her.

Her smile faded. No, better that she hadn't known him then. She would have liked the cocky fighter pilot, but she wouldn't have risked getting to know him. He would have been too much like

Brandon. And her initial delight would have quickly faded away to distrust.

"Grady was telling me that one of the mares is pregnant," she said, as they passed a field filled with frolicking mares and foals.

"She's due in about a month," he said. "Our first birth."

"You sound excited."

"I am. I haven't watched a mare foal since I was a kid."

"I didn't know you were going to start breeding horses."

He turned off the main highway and headed toward the fair grounds where the auction would be held. "I've been thinking about it. When I was little, before I wanted to be a pilot, I always wanted a horse ranch. I know something about blood lines. There's a stallion coming on the market in a few months. I know his owner and I'm going to get first shot to bid. If all goes well, we'll have our own breeding herd in a few years."

Jessie watched him as he spoke. Today was the first day he'd spoken about the ranch without his usual bitterness. She wanted to think that it was her influence on him, but she knew better. Wanting to help him didn't mean that she actually *was* helping him.

They pulled into the parking lot. While Jessie collected her notebook, Mike pulled his Stetson off the seat and set it on his head. They walked toward the crowd milling in the exhibition area. A small well-dressed woman carrying a yappy dog bumped into Jessie, sending her stumbling into Mike. Their hands brushed and he reached up to steady her.

"Sorry," she said. "I was reading my list. I guess I should watch where I'm going."

"Guess you should," he answered, then bent down and brushed her cheek with his mouth.

The quick, soft pressure didn't mean anything, she told herself, even as her heart raced and her palms grew damp. It didn't mean anything at all. So what if she could smell the clean scent of his body and feel his warmth so close to hers? But when a trio of children raced too close to Mike and he was forced to bump into her, she had to fight the urge to huddle close.

"What are we looking for?" he asked as they stepped closer to the furniture on display.

"They're going to have several armoires, a few dressing chests, and possibly some tables for auction." She glanced down at her list. "I don't want to get any of the art work. It'll be too expensive."

"Any chairs?" he asked, pointing at a grouping.

"Nope."

"Good, because those look kinda small and uncomfortable."

As she turned to look where he was pointing, their hands brushed again. He was on her right, so it was his good hand that rested against hers. For a second, she wished she was brave enough to casually slip her fingers between his and then pretend she'd done nothing out of the ordinary. But she wasn't brave.

"Which one?" she asked.

"On the end."

She looked at the small, ornate mahogany chair and then smiled. "If it makes you feel any better, Mike, it's a child's chair. Early Victorian."

"Good, 'cause there was no way I'd fit in that thing."

She laughed, picturing him seated, with his knees up to his chin.

"What's so funny?" he asked, turning toward her.

"You are." Her smile faded as she met his eyes. It would be so easy to get lost in his deep blue irises. Then disappear inside of him and never find her way out.

"Come on," he said, breaking the mood. "There's more to see."

They stopped in front of a selection of armoires. As they studied the pieces of furniture, their arms and hands brushed for the third time. Before she could move away, Mike reached for her hand and linked his fingers with hers. His skin felt warm and alive. She squeezed gently, not daring to look up at him. He returned the pressure.

"What about this piece over here," he said, tugging until she followed him.

Jessie clutched her notebook and smiled. Here she was panting with desire simply because they were holding hands, and all he was interested in was furniture for the ranch.

They moved around the different pieces of furniture, discussing where they would fit in the lodge or cottages. Several times he released her hand to feel the finish on the wood or study the construction, but whenever he was done, he reached for her again. Jessie found herself smiling foolishly at nothing in particular.

Finally, when the auction was about to begin, they went into a large tent set up with chairs. Jessie registered with the cashier, giving them her account information, then went to find where Mike had saved her a seat. He was on the aisle and she slipped in to sit on his right. She was already tired, but he looked ready to walk for miles.

"For someone who hated the ranch as much as you did, you sure are excited about the decorating."

"I never hated the ranch," he said. "I just didn't want to be there now."

She wanted to ask if it was as horrible as he'd thought or if he was getting over his disappointment, but she was afraid of his answer.

As the crowd moved into the tent and filled up the chairs around them, Mike left to get them sodas. When he returned, she took the top can. He popped the top awkwardly with his left hand, then, when he caught her looking, shrugged uncomfortably.

"One day I'll get it right."

"I think you're doing very well," she said. She took a sip and gathered her courage together. "It is getting better, isn't it?"

Mike wanted to pretend he didn't hear the question, but he couldn't do that to Jessie. Besides, he found himself needing to talk about his hand, and she was about the only person he trusted.

"Some." He glanced down at the scars criss-crossing the back of his hand. "I have a little more movement, and I'm working on my fine motor skills."

"What about physical therapy? Would that help?"

"Maybe. There isn't a place close by. The doctors have given me some exercises."

"But you're not doing them."

It wasn't a question. "You don't know that," he said, wondering if he sounded as defensive as he felt.

Jessie turned in her chair until she was facing him. Her brown eyes danced with amusement. "I know."

She wasn't wearing much make-up, but her skin looked as smooth and soft as velvet. Dark hair hung to her shoulders, the thick length swaying with each move of her head. She'd abandoned her jeans and T-shirt for some gauzy red blouse that kept threatening to fall off her shoulders. Twice he'd caught a glimpse of her ivory bra strap. A bright, striped skirt, made of the same material as the blouse, hugged her narrow waist before falling gently over her full hips. She wore sandles on her feet and painted her toes the same color as her blouse. Her perfume surrounded him in a sweetly sensual haze. She was the most feminine creature he had ever known, and as much as he desired her, he felt at ease in her company.

She ran her finger along one of his scars. "How does it feel not to be perfect any more?" she asked.

He started to make a joke, but when she looked up at him, he saw she wasn't kidding. "What do you mean?"

"Oh, look at you, Mike. Good looking, tall, intelligent. You had it all. Now you have to live like the rest of us."

"I was never perfect," he said, giving into temptation and tucking her hair behind her ear. "There were a lot of things I never did well."

"Name one of them."

He could hear the crowd around them, and feel people walking by them to find seats, but it all faded leaving only Jessie and the pleasure of her company. For once, he didn't even mind talking about his former life. "I was never very good with relationships."

"Oh, please." She shook her head. "Grady told me there were women crawling all over you."

"I said relationships, not sex."

She drew her brows together. "If I ask about Pam will you bite my head off?"

"No." He smiled slightly. Her full lips curved up in return. "She is a model, mostly lingerie for catalogues."

Jessie grimaced. "Yuck."

"Pam's very nice."

"I'm sure she is, but I would never want to be friends with a lingerie model. Talk about feeling inadequate and over-blown." She glanced down at her chest. "She was probably a perfect 34B."

Mike leaned close to her. "More like a 32A," he whispered. "I couldn't find them in the dark."

"You are wicked." She laughed. "You thought she was stunning, so don't try to tell me otherwise."

"She was pretty," he admitted. "But we were never close. The relationship was convenient for both of us."

"Oh, Mike, I'm sorry." She touched his arm.

He thought about kissing her, but before he could act on the impulse he felt someone standing behind him.

"Jessica Ross, I thought it was you."

He felt Jessie stiffen as she looked up. "Sandra, how nice to see you."

Mike looked up at a well-preserved matron dressed in tailored slacks and a jacket. Her blond hair was artfully arranged to show off her smooth face. She looked about forty, so he guessed she had to be pushing fifty.

"Sandra Alanthorpe, this is Mike Coburn. He owns the ranch I'm decorating."

"Ma'am," he said, tipping his hat and hoping it was going do be enough. He didn't want to have to shake hands with this woman, or go to the trouble of explaining why he couldn't.

Apparently Sandra Alanthorpe was as taken with him as he was with her because she gave him a vague smile and clutched her program closer to her chest.

"I was just telling Mildred we never see you any more, darling. How are you doing?"

"Fine," Jessie answered. "I've been busy with work."

"Oh, that's right. You have some decorating that you do." She motioned around the tent. "That must be what brings you here. Well, I'm off." She bent over and kissed the air beside Jessie's cheek. "Do keep in touch. We'll have lunch." She waved her arm. "Soon, darling. Ta."

Jessie flopped back in her seat and closed her eyes. Her lips moved, but she wasn't saying anything.

"What are you doing?" he asked.

"Counting to a hundred. It keeps me calm." She folded her arms over her chest and shuddered.

"She's just some over-blown woman with too much money and too much time. Don't let her get to you."

Jessie opened one eye and looked at him. "You sound as if you're familiar with the type."

He grimaced. "I am. I went to a lot of parties at the invitation of women like her."

She opened both eyes and sat straight in her chair. "Then you know why I would never fit in there. Did you see how she looked at what I was wearing? As if she wouldn't use this blouse to dust her cat's litter box?" She sounded outraged. "All those pale-skinned beauties with their light hair and tiny little figures."

Mike grinned. "I like dark hair and eyes and big—"

She turned to look at him. "Big. You mean fat."

"I mean perfect." He put his arm around her shoulders and drew her close to him. She held herself stiffly for a moment, then sagged against him.

At the front of the tent, a man approached the podium. "They're starting," Mike said.

"Good." She still sounded cranky.

Mike smiled, then kissed the top of her head. When she started to sit up, he held her in place. She sighed softly and snuggled close to him.

He wanted to keep her here with him. He wanted to hold her forever. He understood the pain of not fitting in. He knew about the frustration of trying to belong when you had no place to go. He knew about wanting to escape from everything.

Right now, she was his escape. With Jessie he could forget the past and ignore the future. She shifted and he felt her breast brush against his chest. Low in his belly heat stirred to life. He wanted her. He wanted to bury himself in her lush curves and let her body heal them both.

It was about more than passion, he thought with some surprise. It was about trust. He didn't just like Jessica Layton Ross. He trusted her.

"I can't believe you paid eight hundred dollars for that table," Jessie said as they collected their receipts and headed for the truck.

"I thought you'd be happy."

"It's your money."

"I was doing it for you," he said, grinning down at her. "Did you notice who else was bidding for it?"

"Yes." She smiled. "Sandra Alanthorpe. She did get into a snit after you beat her. Did you see how she glared at you when she stalked out?"

The crowd pushed them close together. Jessie reached for his hand. When her fingers touched his, he stiffened but didn't pull away. At first, she was surprised. Didn't he want to hold hands with her anymore? But then she realized she was holding his right hand. She hesitated, torn between pretending nothing was wrong and casually pulling back. Mike decided the situation for her when he gave her a rakish grin and kept on walking.

She hadn't realized she'd been holding her breath until she let it go. She laughed because it was the end of a perfect day.

"All right," she said, as they approached the truck. "I do thank you for buying that table, but you still spent too much."

He opened the truck door and waited until she slid onto the seat. Before she turned to face front, he touched her arm. "I know it's only five, but there's a great restaurant down the road. Would you like to stop for dinner? It's a historic old mill that was turned into an inn. I think you'd like the place."

Was he asking her to dinner, or to something more personal? Jessie stared at Mike. She couldn't see his eyes, so she reached up and pulled off his hat. Now she could see the fire that burned in his blue irises. Desire tightened the lines of his mouth. His words invited her to dinner, but his body asked for something very different.

"I'm not very hungry," she said softly.

Disappointment clouded the fire. She took both his hands in hers and tugged until he stepped right up against the cab. She parted her knees and slid to the edge of the seat. Her full skirt kept her from flashing the people around them, but through the thin material, she could feel his warm thighs and the denim of his jeans.

She wasn't hungry, but she wanted to be with him. She wanted to heal him, and love him.

She blinked, shocked at her own train of thought. Love him? She closed her eyes briefly. Of course. It all made sense now. But why did she have to be drawn to broken men she couldn't heal?

"I'm not hungry," she repeated. "But I would like to see the inn."

He bent close and kissed her mouth. As his lips touched hers, as his left hand buried itself in her hair, she fought against a wave of pain.

Seven months ago, when he was still a pilot and considered himself whole, he would not have chosen her. When he was healed and considered himself whole once again, he would let her go. She only had this short time in between to claim him.

When he was done with her, she would walk away without ever letting him know that as he took her body, she willingly surrendered her heart.

Twelve

Their room was large, with a fireplace and king-sized bed. Floral wallpaper matched the quilted comforter. Lace curtains filtered the late afternoon sunlight. Jessie wondered if she should offer to close the blinds. She bit her lower lip and stared at the center of Mike's shirt. They were standing close enough to touch. Close enough that she could feel his heat and his nervousness. Part of her wanted to tell him she'd changed her mind. Part of her would perish if they didn't make love.

The silence around them grew, broken only by the soft ticking of a clock on the mantel. She could hear their breathing, faint, too fast, and shallow.

"I'm scared," she whispered at last.

Mike touched her chin and forced her to look at him. His eyes darkened with concern and need. "Why?"

"I haven't been with anyone since Brandon passed away."

"I haven't been with anyone since the accident."

"What if we've forgotten how?"

He smiled faintly. "I haven't forgotten."

The bed was behind her. She collapsed on it, sitting on the edge. "Mike, I'm terrified I'll say something or do something to make you angry. I don't mean to beat a dead horse here, but what about your hand?"

He flushed and started to turn away.

She grabbed him by the shirtsleeve. "No, wait. That's not what I meant. I'm asking you to please understand if I do something stupid. You know how I am when I get nervous, and I'm really nervous."

He swallowed hard. "I won't be angry."

She gently touched his injured hand, then drew it close to her. "Can you feel anything?"

"I can feel you touching me."

She studied his long fingers, and the scars marring his male beauty. She traced one long, thin line around the base of his thumb. She bent down and touched the scar with her tongue.

He drew in a sharp breath. "I can feel that."

"Does it feel good?" she asked, not daring to look at him.

"Yes."

She continued to caress his hand, loving each tiny imperfection. She drew his fingers into her mouth, one by one. He tasted faintly salty. As she sucked on his forefinger, she saw his erection straining against the fly of his jeans. When she had tended to every part of his hand, she placed it against her breast and looked up at him.

"Make love to me," she whispered.

He drew her to her feet. "You are an incredible woman."

"No." She shook her head. "I'm just Jessie."

He pulled her hard against him and claimed her mouth. She opened to him instantly, wanting his tongue to mate with hers. Her breasts flattened against his chest, and she wrapped her arms around him.

She needed this, she thought as the fire in her chest and between her thighs flared to life. She needed to be held and loved by this man. He cupped her face and stared into her eyes. When she smiled at him, he traced her mouth with his thumb.

"God, I need you," he murmured, and reached for her blouse.

There were no buttons this time. She wasn't sure why she'd chosen this particular outfit. Had she hoped they would make love or was it a stroke of luck that he could pull her blouse over her head and slip her skirt down her hips? Her bra opened with an easy flick of his fingers. She shrugged out of the lacy garment.

As he stared at her, she fought the urge to cover herself. She wasn't perfect. Her breasts weren't as perky as they had been when she'd been a teenager, and her stomach had never been flat. She wondered how beautiful and perfect Pam had been.

Then Mike sank to his knees and slowly pulled off her panties. He kissed her stomach and rubbed his hands up and down her thighs. She tried to figure out if she could tell the difference between his good and bad hand, but when he slipped one finger between her thighs and touched her waiting heat, she realized it didn't matter at all.

He urged her to sit on the bed and quickly removed his clothing. When he stood before her naked, he was more beautiful than she'd imagined. Long lean lines, broad shoulders that tapered to a narrow waist. Gold blond hair sparsely covered his chest, angling down to a single line that stretched past his belly before widening at the apex of his thighs. His erection strained toward her.

Before she could touch him, he walked around to the other side of the bed and pulled back the covers. She joined him on the white sheets, loving the contrast of the cool cotton and the heated flesh of her body. She lay on her back. He was next to her, his head propped up on his hand. He stared at her for so long, she wondered if something was wrong.

"Don't get worried," he said, reading her expression. "I like looking at you."

"Why?"

He smiled. "You're very beautiful."

"Liar."

His smiled faded. "Sweet Jessie, you are the most perfect woman I know."

"You're just saying that because I have breasts."

"What breasts," he asked, playfully, never taking his gaze from her face.

"These." She raised her chest slightly.

"Take my hand and show me."

Jessie stared at him. Okay, she was officially out of her league. Making love with Brandon had always been pleasurable. He carefully brought her to orgasm, then pleased himself. It had been a civilized coupling that rarely took longer than twelve minutes. They hadn't talked much, had never played. Brandon had been her first and only lover.

"You can do it," Mike encouraged. He raised his left hand and placed it on her stomach.

She reached down for his wrist and drew his hand up until it covered one of her breasts.

He looked faintly disappointed. "That's it?"

"What do you want from me?" she asked, embarrassed and confused.

"Oh, baby, the question is what do you want from me?"

He bent down and kissed her. With his tongue he traced the shape of her mouth, circling around until the nerves in her lips hummed. He dipped inside and touched the very tip of her tongue. Point to point, they moved against each other.

Her breasts swelled. His hand squeezed slightly, then pressed down. She moaned.

He raised his head. "You like that?"

"Yes."

"What else?"

This time it was easier to take his hand and move it on her body. She'd never explored herself this way, so she found her sensitive spots along with him. She drew his palm over her hardening nipples. She paused to let his fingers play there. He brought his head down and suckled her. Lightning bolts of need shot through her, making her raise her hips and flex her muscles.

When he had trailed kisses along her chest and down her belly, she found the courage to draw his hand lower, until he touched between her thighs. His fingers sought and found her sweet spot, circling it, slipping through the damp curls, then moving away, only to return seconds later.

Having him touch her like that was almost enough to cause her to explode. Just as she was reaching for ecstasy, he removed his hand and sat up.

Lazily, she opened her eyes. "Was it something I said?"

"No." He smiled and bent over the side of the bed. Seconds later he straightened and handed her a foil packet. "Would you care to do the honors?"

A condom. She stared at it. Of course, she thought, grateful he'd though of protection. He wanted her to put it on him. She stared from the package to him.

"What's wrong?" he asked.

"I've never seen one of these before."

He stared down at her and started to laugh.

"It's not funny."

"Yes, it is," he said, and rolled onto his back.

She told herself she was insulted, even as her mouth quivered. Pretty soon, she was laughing with him. She bent over and kissed his shoulder, then bit down on his skin. His laughter turned into a moan. He smelled clean and male, and tasted like heaven. Clutching the package in one hand, she braced herself over him and explored his chest with her mouth. She traced circles around his flat nipples, and teased the blond hair arrowing down his belly. She reached up and kissed his mouth, then the strong line of his jaw, where his five o'clock shadow scraped delightfully against her swollen mouth.

She raised her head and studied his face. Words of love hovered on her tongue, but she held them back. His blue eyes met and held hers.

"Did you mean what you said about never having seen a condom before?"

She nodded, fighting a blush.

"I don't think I can put it on one-handed, Jessie."

"Oh." She bit her lower lip. "Okay, I'll do it."

She moved to kneel between his thighs and opened the package. She stared from the rolled up protection to his erection. "This isn't going to work."

He propped himself up on one elbow and grinned. "It stretches."

"It better stretch a lot."

Before slipping it on, she touched him. His shaft was hard and warm against her hand. She closed her eyes and savored the feel of him, all sleek strength and male power.

"Jessie? You'd better stop that."

"Why?" She opened her eyes and looked at him. The heat of his desire burned through to her soul.

"It's been a long time, and I don't have that much control."

"Oh." She placed the protection over him and gently rolled it down. She could feel her cheeks flaming, but she concentrated on the task at hand and not her own embarrassment. When she was done, she sat back on her heels and studied her handiwork. "I like it." A forbidden image filled her mind. She stared at the white sheets. "Would you mind if I was, you know . . ."

"What?"

She took a deep breath and blurted it out very quickly. "Could I be on top? I've always wanted to be, and well, it might be easier and if you don't mind, I'd sortta like it and . . ."

"Jessie?"

"Yeah?" She couldn't look at him.

"Come here. I want to hold you and bury myself in you. And yes, you can be on top."

She covered her face with her hands. "I can't now."

"Why not?"

"I'm shy!"

He chuckled, then pulled her close. After kissing her senseless, he helped her until she was straddling him. She felt him probing at her moist center, then he clutched her hips and drew her back over him. Slowly, he filled her. Her gaze held his and she watched as pleasure darkened his eyes.

They moved slowly together. Her breasts bounced against her chest. She wanted to hold them still until she saw him watching them. "So beautiful," he murmured.

He played with her nipples, all the while his thrusts built up pressure inside of her. She felt herself moving quickly toward her release.

He dropped one of his hands and slipped his thumb between their bodies. He touched her sweet spot.

Instantly, her world shifted and spun out of control. He raised his hips higher and touched something deep inside of her. Her muscles quivered then shook with a million ripples of sensation. She called out his name and heard an answering response as his body surged under hers. Their individual orgasms fed each other, sending them higher and higher until all they could do was cling to each other, panting in spent ecstasy.

It was almost a half hour later before Mike felt the need to move. Jessie had curled up next to him, her thigh over his, her knee nestling against his groin. Their hands laced together on his belly. Outside, the afternoon had slipped away to evening, and the room had grown dark. But he didn't need to see her to know how beautiful she was.

He turned his head and kissed her hair. Her scent drifted to him, the spicy fragrance now laced with the musky overtones of their passion. Her body felt feminine and welcoming next to his. Lazily he stroked her skin. Soft, he thought smiling slightly. So damn soft.

She sighed with contentment and snuggled closer. Inside his chest, he felt a swelling of pride. He'd pleased her. His hand hadn't mattered at all. His smile grew broader as he remembered the look on her face when she'd opened the package containing the condom and stared from the protection to him, and back. So shy, yet so willing to try anything. He liked making love with her.

He stared at the ceiling. Had he ever make love *with* someone before? He thought about his past, about the women who had come on to him in bars and at parties. They had been the ones making all the moves. He'd simply gone along for the ride. It was enough that he show up in bed hard; they'd taken care of the rest of it. He'd pleased them, he remembered, but mostly out of ego rather than caring. Today had been different. He'd wanted to please Jessie because he needed to see her raw and vulnerable. Because if he didn't view her passionate ecstasy, if he didn't hear her cries and feel her explode beneath him, he could not continue on.

It scared the hell out of him. It made him want to make love to her again.

He shifted slightly, sliding out from under her leg. When she protested, he kissed her gently, savoring the taste and texture of her willing mouth. He trailed kisses down her throat and when she murmured that she was completely sated, he suckled on her breasts until she squirmed beneath him.

As her hands clutched at his shoulders, he slipped his fingers lower, across her soft belly, down through her damp curls. He found her most sensitive place and loved it until she was panting with need, her eyes unfocused, her body his to command. Then he brought her to completion, watching her give in to the passion, selfishly needing to hear his name on her lips. He kissed her breasts and moved his fingers until she could only lay limply in his arms—spent and quivering. He ignored his own erection, content to hold her. For the first time in his life, he was happy to have been the one giving.

He was concerned that she would misunderstand the gesture and reach for him, but Jessie had always read him better than he read himself. She snuggled close again, her body slick with perspiration.

"You were right," she whispered, her breath warm against his chest.

"I'm always right. What about this time?"

He felt her mouth pull into a smile. "That all the important parts of you are working fine. You should have warned me you were such a good lover."

A good lover. He'd never thought about it one way or the other. He'd always been a fighter pilot. Then an ex-fighter pilot. Today Jessie had introduced him as a rancher. Now he was her lover.

She raised up on one elbow and looked down at him. Emotions chasing through her dark eyes. Sated passion, contentment, and something else he didn't want to name.

Panic flared. "Don't," he said, turning away. "Don't care about me."

"All right," she said. From the tone of her voice, she was calm, but he didn't dare look at her. He didn't want to see the hurt on her face.

"Jessie, I'm sorry. I didn't mean that. I just—"

"Don't worry, Mike. I wasn't about to declare my undying love for you." She laughed.

He hated the harsh, brittle sound and moved back toward her. "Jessie, I'm trying to save you heartache. I'm not who you think."

She'd pulled the sheet up to her shoulders and was leaning against the wood headboard. Her hair tumbled to her shoulders. She looked rumpled and sexy, as if she'd just made love. But her eyes accused him of playing with her emotions.

He leaned close to her and reached out to touch her cheek. She jerked her head away from him. "What's the story, Mike? Are you afraid that I'll become one of the groupies and hang around you like a love-sick teenager?" She raised her eyebrows. "Don't sweat it. The sex was hot, I can't deny that, but I know how to play this game with the best of them. What was it you said before? It's just a roll in the hay. This time we used sheets." She shrugged. "Same thing."

She swung her legs over the side of the bed and started to get up. He could feel her pain and embarrassment as if it were his own.

He slid across the bed and caught her arm. When he pulled, she resisted, but he was stronger. He jerked again and she tumbled backwards onto the mattress. Her beautiful hair fanned out over the white sheets. She wouldn't look at him. He touched her chin and forced him to meet her gaze. The tears swimming there ripped at his heart.

"I'm a complete bastard," he said.

She sniffed. "You're preaching to the choir, here. You're not going to get any argument from me."

"Hate me, Jessie. Hate and despise me, because that's what I deserve."

She tilted her chin up in defiance. Lord, he admired her, he thought, waiting for her to say she did despise him. Naked in bed with him, she still had the courage to mock him.

"I can't," she whispered, and looked away. A single tear rolled down her face.

He released her and sat on the edge of the bed with his back to her. He stared at his scarred hand, but instead of flesh and bone, he saw the deck of the carrier and the jets preparing for take-off. A few minutes ago, he had pleased Jessie because he wanted to know that he could. She might perceive it as a selfless gesture, but he knew the motivation behind the act. This time, however, he would tell her the truth. He would expose his darkest secret, so that she could walk away. It sounded noble, but the truth was, he couldn't bear to have her stay. He couldn't risk caring about anything ever again. He had nothing to give her, nothing to offer. If he waited too long, he wouldn't want her to go. When she knew the truth, she would run from him and he would be alone. It would be better for both of them.

"I don't know how much Grady told you about the accident," he said, wondering if she could feel the deck moving and taste the sea spray.

"Not much," she said.

"We hadn't been at sea more than a couple of weeks," he said, fighting against the memories. "Tim Evans was just a kid. Eighteen, I think. He'd never been away from home before. There were a hundred like him on the ship. Young, scared, puking their guts out and wanting to go home. He got in the way of a jet. The pilot was about to start the engines. He would have been fried by the exhaust. I grabbed him." Mike stared down at his hand and flexed it. "I jerked him out of the way. He was heavier than he looked and to keep my balance, I put my hand on a metal support. Seconds later, a hydraulic door closed on it." Funny, he could remember the sound of his screams, but he couldn't feel the pain anymore. The only blessing, he thought grimly.

He heard Jessie's sharp intake of breath. He went on before she could speak. "They opened it quickly, but the damage had been done." Now, instead of his fine network of scars he saw the broken skin and crushed bone, a bloody mass of tissue hanging at the end of his arm.

"They flew me to their best specialist. Two days later, when I realized what had happened, he came to see me."

"Tim?" she asked.

He nodded. Now he would tell her the part even Grady didn't know. He would speak the words and she would be gone from his life. He rose from his feet and walked to the fireplace. The last flickering flames cast shadows on the walls.

"He came to apologize. I wouldn't listen." He shut his eyes, but he could still see the boy standing in front of him, still hear his sobs. "I told him I would never forgive him. He was some hick farm kid. I was a Top Gun fighter pilot. I told him I should have let him die in the jet wash. I told him if I had it to do again, I would let him die."

His words hovered in the room, growing larger and larger, taking on a life of their own. He stared into the fire and waited for her gasp of shock, waited for the disgust he would hear in her voice.

"You don't mean that," she said at last, sounding surprisingly normal.

Denial. It made sense. Jessie would want to deny that kind of ugliness. "I meant it when I said it to his face, and I mean it today. If I had it to do all over again, I would let that kid die."

Thirteen

Jessie wanted to run away. She wanted to cover her ears and not hear the horrible words, but it was too late for that. They filled her mind. Loud words, firmly imprinted on her memory. She didn't believe him; he couldn't mean it. But he'd said it. And that changed everything.

Even as she wondered if she could gather her clothes together and escape before he caught her, she rose to her feet and walked toward him. He stood with his back to the room, staring at the dying fire.

He was the most beautiful man she had ever seen. Like some living statue, the sleek lines of his body were frozen in a moment of pain. She felt it, could taste it. Bitter regret and shame. He might claim to want Tim Evan's life as forfeit for his own suffering, but he hated himself for the wish, even as he believed it was true.

Everyone carried black spots on their souls. She, too, had confessions she could make. They were more undefined than Mike's, feelings of inadequacy, of not being enough, of having failed her husband, and perhaps even herself. She had never had the courage to speak them. Even though Mike has used his darkness to scare her away, he could not have done it easily. Not after what they had just shared.

She touched his hip. His skin was warm beneath her fingers. He flinched slightly, but did not turn. She traced the line to his waist, then up across his back. He shuddered as if her light caress brought him untold pain. She took another step toward him, and rested her body against his. She brought her hands up around him, pulling him until they touched firmly. Her fingers discovered his chest and ribs.

She longed to tell him that she loved him, but he would not hear the words, only the compassion. He would assume it was pity that caused her to take his hand now, and lead him back to their bed. He would question why she slipped under the sheets and drew him next to her, and he would not understand why she covered his body with her own, as if her heat, her love and concern, could heal him.

They lay on the bed for several minutes before she leaned over and switched on the bedside light. The bulb illuminated the planes of his face. She outlined his eyebrows and his mouth with her fingers.

"I know you believe what you've told me," she said. "But I don't. Shh." She touched her hand to his mouth when he would have spoken. "You are strong and brave. I have watched you struggle to relearn the simplest tasks. I admire your courage in that, and in telling me about Tim. You can't scare me away that easily, Mike." She smiled and wondered why he was getting blurry. It wasn't until a tear fell on his cheek that she realized she was crying.

"Damn it, Jessie, don't." He brushed her cheeks. "I'm not worth it. Haven't you figured that out yet?"

"No."

She kissed him. He resisted at first, holding his mouth closed against her own. Then she whispered his name, catching it on a sob. He groaned and parted his lips to admit her.

He tasted salty from her tears. Beneath her body, she felt him stirring to life. He rolled her onto her back and reached for the protection. This time she worked quickly, then guided him into her.

He thrust once, deeply, then gathered her close and held her as if she was his last chance at life. She clung to him, savoring the weight of his body on hers. Her tears flowed down her temples and into her hair.

When he raised up, she reached for his right hand. She kissed the scars and washed them with her tears, as if she had a magic power to cure him. He moved against her quickly now, and she flexed her hips. Her body stirred, but not enough, and before she could catch up, he plunged in deeply and stiffened. He spoke her name like a prayer.

Later, when he slept, she stared into the darkness and searched for an answer. She was sinking in well past her depth. She didn't know what to do about Mike or herself.

She traced the hand holding hers. It was his right. She could feel the bumps and ridges from his surgeries. This hand could tame a horse, throw a rope, and pleasure a woman. These fingers—she outlined them—long and elegant, strong and scarred, could not write easily, couldn't manipulate a jet control stick with sufficient finesse.

She turned his hand over. This palm, rough, callused, broad. All mismatched parts of an imperfect whole. If not for this hand, his life would have continued. If not for this hand, she would never have met Mike, never have known him. If not for this hand, she would never have loved him.

While Mike raged against fate and wished Tim Evans dead, Jessie realized her own dark secret was that she was grateful for the circumstances that had brought them together. She couldn't imagine what her life would be like if she'd never known him. A fierceness swept through her and she moved closer to him.

In his sleep he wrapped his arm around her and rested his chin on her hair. She listened to the sound of his heart. She would do anything for him, if only he would ask.

She closed her eyes and thought of the letter that had been delivered that morning. Tim's mother loved her son. Jessie hadn't read the words, but she could imagine the woman's pleas. The young man must be suffering terribly.

Jessie willed herself to sleep, all the while she struggled to find an answer to the problem. It was her nature to fix that which was broken. Only this time, the solution eluded her. It had to be there, she told herself but it wasn't.

She'd been wrong a moment ago. Her dark secret wasn't that she was glad to have this time with Mike. Her secrets was far worse. She couldn't protect Brandon from himself, and now she couldn't heal Mike. She was incapable of saving anyone she loved.

On the morning of their third day at the inn, Jessie woke before dawn. She pulled an extra blanket off the bed and wrapped it around herself. She quietly opened the blinds and settled in the window seat to watch the sun rise.

Outside, birds called to each other as the sky slowly lightened from midnight blue to gray to orange. The first full rays were searching across the mountains when Mike woke and joined her. They had only left the inn to buy toiletries and a change of clothing. They had their food delivered to the room. She had become as familiar with his body as with her own.

Now he pulled her onto his lap and hugged her close. His skin smelled of sleep and sex. She nipped at his shoulder, tasting his flavor. Below her hip, he stirred to life.

"We should probably head back," he said.

She nodded. It was time to return to the real world. She didn't want to. She wanted to stay at this inn forever. Being with Mike, loving him, being loved had been the most perfect part of her life. The first morning, when they could have stared at each other with embarrassed awkwardness, he'd simply touched her face and thanked her for staying with him. She smiled and asked where else was she going to go. They'd make love, then, quick and fast, tangling the sheets and blankets until their mutual release sent them back into a restful sleep.

Her body ached from their passion, the soreness a pleasant reminder of shared intimacy. She had never been so thoroughly satisfied, had never felt more desirable or needed.

He shifted on the seat until she was straddling him. As his hands played their games on her body, she raised herself up to take him inside. They rode out the storm together, and when their heartbeats and breathing had returned to normal, they clung to each other, as if both dared not be the first to let go.

On the drive back to the ranch, Jessie chatted about the furniture that they'd bought at the auction.

"It should have been delivered by now," she said, studying the scenery around them. "I'll store it downstairs. The painters will be done, as well. The wallpaper people should be here at the end of the week, and then the carpet is being laid."

"It's all coming together."

She couldn't tell if he was enthused or simply being polite and she didn't want to know. They were almost at the ranch. What would happen now? Had these three days been a dream? Would everything go back to the way it had been, or would Mike want something more?

And what did she want? Jessie bit her lower lip as he drove the truck down the familiar long driveway. Maybe it was weak and spineless, but she wanted it all. She wanted to spend the rest of her life like she'd spent the last few days. She wanted to be with Mike and love him; she wanted to be free to touch him and be touched; she wanted to listen to his breathing as he slept and feel the warmth of his body next to hers every morning.

If that wasn't possible, she wanted to share the short time they had left.

Mike stopped the truck in front of his house. "We're here."

"Yeah." Jessie reached for her purse and the bag containing her dirty clothes. She opened the door and stepped out. She'd half-expected Grady to come out to greet them, but the old man didn't appear.

She looked up at Mike, but didn't know what to say. She told herself she could ask if she could stay with him, but even as the thought appeared, she dismissed it. She wasn't the type to be that bold.

"I'd better get back to my place," she said, holding up the bag of belongings. "Change my clothes and go to work."

He nodded and fell into step beside her. She wanted him to speak, but he was silent. When they reached the trailer, she turned and smiled at him.

"Thanks for everything. I really had a good time."

He took off his Stetson and rotated it in his hands. His blue eyes met and held hers. "Don't go, Jessie."

Her heart leapt in her chest. What was he saying? How long did he want her to stay? She looked at him and willed him to say the words.

"Stay with me at the house. Until the job is done."

A temporary arrangement. The disappointment crashed through her, and she struggled to keep him from seeing it in her face. She had hoped for a little more. Don't be foolish, she told herself. What had she expected? A marriage proposal?

Even as she tried to deny it to herself, she knew that was exactly what she'd been hoping for. She had hoped Mike had figured out that he loved her and wanted her with him always.

"I know I haven't been the easiest man in the world to get along with," he said, and shrugged. "I'll try to do better. It's just—" He drew in a deep breath. "I need you Jessie. You make me feel whole."

It wasn't love, but it was close, she thought, as she smiled up at him. It was so much more than Brandon had wanted. Not once in all the time they'd dated or been married had he ever needed her for anything. He'd let her decorate his penthouse apartment because it gave her something to do. He had full-time help, so she hadn't had to cook dinner. His secretary gave better parties than she did. Even in bed he'd never really needed her. He'd make love to her with the same regularity and dedication he showed to his four times a week work-out with his personal trainer. How she'd longed to hear that she was needed.

"It'll just take me a minute to pack," she said and stepped into the trailer.

Jessie hovered in the hallway for as long as she could, then she forced herself to move into the kitchen. This was worse than the time her mother had caught her necking in the living room with a boy from high school. She imagined Grady and Mrs. McGregor would both be scandalized by the fact that she'd moved in with Mike. She wished she knew if he'd warned them.

She could feel her cheeks flame as she crossed the threshold. Mrs. McGregor was at the stove cooking breakfast, while Grady and Mike sat at the table. Last night, she and Mike had gone into town for dinner and had gotten back after Grady had gone to bed. There had been no one to witness their giggling conversation as they'd argued over whether or not he could carry her up the stairs. If her foot hitting the wall and their muffled laughter had awakened the older man, he hadn't bothered coming out of his room. Later, there had been only quiet murmurs and soft moans as they had shared their bodies with each other long into the night.

Jessie quietly grabbed a mug and reached for the coffee pot. The machine hissed as she picked it up and Grady glanced at her.

She stood frozen, like a child caught stealing from the cookie jar. Before she could gather her scattered thoughts together he nodded to the empty chair on his left.

"Morning, little lady. The painters are finishing up the trim today."

"Good morning," she mumbled, pouring her coffee. Grady sounded normal. Maybe he didn't know. Maybe no one knew. Maybe they just thought she was coming in for breakfast. As she approached the table, that hope was dashed by the sight of a third place setting. Mike looked up and winked. She smiled back. As she went to step past him, he grabbed her around the waist and pulled her close.

"I tried to be quiet when I got up," he said and kissed her cheek. "I thought you might like to sleep late."

So much for everyone not knowing. "I'm fine," she said and took the empty chair. Mrs. McGregor served up the eggs and bacon and gave everyone a plate. When their eyes met, the older woman winked at her before scolding Grady for putting on hot sauce when he hadn't even tasted the food.

Jessie stared at the sunlit room and the three familiar people talking together. They had accepted her and her relationship with Mike. She remembered how Brandon's friends had ignored her and her friends had abandoned her. For the first time in her life, she felt as if she belonged. Smiling, she picked up her fork and started eating her breakfast.

When they were done with the meal, Grady took them out into the barn and showed them the new horses that had been delivered. A gray stood in one stall. Farther down were two bays and a palomino. All geldings.

"We got us another fine mare," he said, pointing to the last stall. "It's almost her time, but I think we should wait another month or so before breeding her."

He and Mike discussed which of the two stallions should cover her, then went through the list of college students still waiting for interviews. Jessie leaned against one of the stalls and patted the horse inside. She should get back to her work. She'd been gone three days. But somehow she couldn't stir herself. She'd rather stay here and watch Mike.

This morning he moved easily through the stable, pointing out things that needed to be done, going over tack and figuring out which horses would do for which kind of riders. Later, when the two men headed for the lodge, she trailed along, smiling when Mike took her hand, and laughing at one of Grady's awful jokes.

"I've been thinking about building a small arena," Mike said, pausing at the lodge's porch steps. "We could sponsor a local rodeo, maybe in August or September."

Grady scratched his head. "Might be worth a try. They're getting to be more and more popular. Could have a special week that ended in the rodeo. Maybe an amateur event on Saturday, and the pro's on Sunday."

But Mike wasn't paying attention. He was looking up at the sky. Jessie followed his gaze. She couldn't see anything, but she heard a distance sound. An airplane traveling at high speed.

"An old one," he said. "Maybe an A-5."

At last she could see a tiny speck moving toward the mountains. In a few minutes it was out of sight and the sound faded shortly after that. Jessie turned to Mike, ready to make a comment about the rodeo. He was still looking up. Slowly, he lowered his head. All the animation had fled his eyes, leaving behind stark pain and a longing so strong, she thought she would die from his need. He absently rubbed his right hand with his left, then spun on his heel and walked down the stairs and toward the barn.

She thought about going after him, but she had nothing to say. Besides, she had her own demons to wrestle with. She knew he might enjoy the ranch, but that it would always be second best in his eyes. No matter how successful he became, he would always remember that he had been denied his first love. And each time a jet flew overhead, he would remember what it had been like to conquer the skies. This beautiful haven was still a prison, and like the ranch itself, Jessie knew that compared with Pam, she, too, was second best.

"Why me?" she asked Grady, two weeks later.

He held out the envelope with its midwestern postmark. "Because you're the only one he'll listen to."

She took the envelope and stared at it. "It's already open."

He shrugged. "I didn't think you'd feel comfortable reading someone else's mail, so I read it first."

"That's supposed to make me feel better?" She stared at the folded sheet of paper. "I can't do this."

"Then I'll read it to you." He snatched back the letter and unfolded it. After scanning the contents, he said, "It's from the boy's mama. She says her son is fading away from the guilt of what he's done. He won't eat or sleep. He's supposed to be on leave, but he won't see any of his friends. She says that—"

Jessie grabbed the letter from him and stared at the neat handwriting. "I can't do this, Grady. I can't change the way Mike feels about Tim Evans."

"You can make him listen. All he has to do is see the boy one time. Let him apologize, accept the apology and send him off with a smile."

"That will never happen," she said, and stared out of the suite bedroom window toward the corral. The lodge was almost finished. She had spent the morning sorting through the prints and paintings she'd purchased and hanging them in the different rooms. Tomorrow she would supervise the painting in the cottages. They would be finished by the end of next week. The following Saturday the guests would begin to arrive. Her job would be done, and she wouldn't have any excuse to stay. Unless Mike asked her to.

"You're the only one," Grady said, sounding as ornery and stubborn as a mule. "You have to set this thing right. It's why you were sent here, Jessie, and you know it."

She smiled at the old man. "I didn't know sailors believed in that sort of thing."

"You spend enough time at sea, you start to believe in a lot of things. You love the boy. I see it in your eyes every time you look at him."

But does he love me? She didn't bother asking the question for two reasons. First, she didn't think Grady had an answer. Second, if he did, she had a feeling it wasn't the answer she wanted to hear.

"All right," she said, holding the letter tightly in her hand. "I'll go talk to him. Ignore the screams you hear from the corral."

"You're a good woman," Grady said and gave her a quick hug.

She appreciated his support even as she wondered if what he'd asked her to do would be the end of her relationship with Mike. Despite their physical closeness, there were some things they never discussed. It was as if he'd never made his confession about Tim Evans. It was her fault, she supposed. She could have pushed the issue several times, but had always backed off. Looks like she wasn't going to get that chance again.

Mike was working a bay gelding when Jessie approached. Pleased to see her, he dismounted and walked over to the railing. It had warmed up enough for her to wear shorts. She tanned quickly in the late spring weather, and her white shorts showed off her legs to perfection. A bright red tank top left her arms bare. She'd tied her hair back with a multi-colored scarf. Red and white earrings hung almost to her shoulders. She moved with the easy grace of a woman who is comfortable in her own skin. Just watching her made him remember how they'd pleasured each other the previous night. Since Jessie had started sharing his bed, he no longer had the dreams of landing on the aircraft carrier. However, their love making kept him up past midnight, so he wasn't getting any more sleep.

He grinned as she approached. It seemed like a fair exchange. "How'd you know I was thinking about you?" he asked, when she got within hearing distance.

"I didn't," she said, not returning his smile.

"What's wrong, Jessie?"

She hesitated a second, then thrust him a letter. He stared at it and recognized the handwriting. It was like being doused with a bucket of water. His desire and good humor fled instantly, leaving behind dangerous anger and threatening rage.

"No," he said, turning away and leading the gelding back to the barn.

"He only wants to talk to you." She followed behind.

"I have nothing to say to him."

"Then listen while he talks. Please, Mike. You have to do this. It's an important part of your healing. You won't be able to move on."

"Thanks for the insight, Dr. Layton, but when I want a professional opinion about my psyche, I'll call in a psychiatrist."

When he reached the barn, he secured the horse and began unbuckling the saddle. Jessie hovered next to him. "If you would just read the letter."

"No."

"All he wants to do is make sure he didn't destroy your life."

"All? That's all?" He lifted off the saddle and carried it into the tack room. Control, he muttered to himself. He had to keep control. But he could feel the anger burning hotter and hotter. Of all people, she should know what she was asking of him.

She was still standing by the horse when he returned. Mike grabbed the letter from her and tore it into several pieces. "He did destroy my life, Jessie. Every damn bit of it. I guess you weren't listening before when I told you how I felt about Tim Evans. I would gladly live that moment over again and let the kid die if it meant I could fly again."

Her dark eyes held his. "I don't believe you."

She sounded so damn convinced. "Don't try to save me, babe, I'm long past rescuing."

"I'm not saving you. I'm telling the truth."

He laughed harshly. "What makes you such an expert on Mike Coburn?"

She raised up her chin defiantly. "The fact that I love you."

He hadn't known how much he wanted to hear the words until she said them. But to speak them now, like this, to use her affection to bend him to her will. His anger burned even hotter and the rage kicked in. He was about two seconds away from losing it completely.

"Damn it," he growled. "How dare you?"

She couldn't have looked more shocked if he'd spit on her, he thought with some distant rational part of his brain. But it wasn't enough to keep him from saying things he knew he would regret. She'd awakened him, had made him believe, and then she'd twisted everything to come out her way.

"I love you," he said in a mocking voice, clenching his hands into fists. His right hand hurt. He wanted the pain, needed it, so he squeezed his fingers tighter into his palms. "You couldn't get your way, so you resort to that? The ultimate in female manipulation. I expected better from you."

She spun on her heel. The fact that she would walk out on him fueled his fire. He grabbed her arm and held her in place.

"I'm not finished," he said.

"Well, I am." She looked up at him, and tried to jerk free. "So now what? How long are you going to hold me here? You want to punish me, Mike? You want to hurt me some more? Yes, I love you, damn it. It's about the stupidest thing I've ever done. You don't want to believe me, then fine. Go ahead and think I'm manipulating you, if that's what you need to do to feel like a man. Why not? Making you feel like a man is all I'm good for anyway."

If she'd been angry, he wouldn't have believed her, but the sorrow in her eyes convinced him more than any words. He released her. She choked back a sob and rushed out of the barn.

The shame tasted metallic on his tongue. He leaned his head against the gelding and cursed himself. In his sorry life he'd done many awful things. But never had he deliberately hurt someone he cared about. Until today. Until Jessie.

She was right, damn her. He *had* used her to feel like a man. So what did that make him when she left? Would he go back to what he had been? A shell? Half a man?

I love you. Her words echoed over and over in his mind. Lord, he wanted them to be true. But what if they were? What did he have to offer her? She was the majority stockholder in Ross Construction. All he had was this ranch.

He looked down at his hand. If he were still a jet jockey, none of this would matter. He could claim her then. Her money wouldn't matter. He glanced out the open barn door toward the sky. There was no point in wishing for the impossible. He would never fly jets again, and he would never let Jessie know that she had become his whole reason for living.

Fourteen

Jessie didn't bother coming to dinner. Mrs. McGregor served the evening meal, then left for her small house on the edge of town. The third place setting sat unoccupied as he and Grady ate their grilled pork chops, green beans and potatoes. The old man didn't say a word. He didn't have to. Every few minutes he would look from Jessie's place at the table, to Mike, and then back to his plate. It was easy to see whom he blamed for Jessie's absence.

After about ten minutes, Mike pushed away his untouched dinner and rose. He walked into the hallway, not sure where he should go. He hadn't seen Jessie since she'd run from him in the barn. It hurt too much to think about what had happened there, but he couldn't turn off the tape in his head. He hated himself for what he'd done to her. He didn't much care for what he'd done to himself either.

Jessie was the best thing to happen to him in years. Every chance he got, he screwed things up between them. He was so damned scared. Mike stared at his scarred hand, then looked away. If he was any kind of a man, he would simply let her go. It was the noble thing to do. But he'd already figured out he wasn't any kind of man without her, so why should he act like anything other than the bastard that he was?

He walked to the foot of the stairs and wondered if she'd escaped to their shared room or to her trailer. He knew she hadn't left the ranch. Both her van and the Mercedes were parked under the car port. If she was in her trailer, she had left him, emotionally, if not physically. If she was in their bedroom, he still had a chance.

He placed his left hand on the railing and slowly climbed the stairs. He didn't want to find out which it was to be, but his feet carried him to the closed bedroom door. Without knocking, he pushed it open.

Relief swamped him. She sat in the over-stuffed chair in the far corner. The room was a hodge-podge of furniture, the bed, a small writing table, the chair. Nothing matched. He hadn't cared enough to buy anything new or paint the walls. For him, this room was just one more part of the prison. Now, seeing her with her feet pulled up under her, with her thick burgundy robe covering her body, he knew he'd been wrong to let her stay in this drab room. He should have let her decorate it, change the furniture, the carpet. This should have been a room she wanted to come back to at night.

A single light shone in the dark room. The floor lamp behind her illuminated her body while leaving her face in shadow. He wanted to see the expression in her eyes, but he couldn't. The light exposed only him.

She made no move toward him, didn't speak. She might have been asleep, except he could feel her studying him, weighing her options, coming to a decision. He wanted to plead his case, but there was no excuse great enough for her to forgive him. Time after time she gave to him; time after time he hurt her and turned away. One day he would turn her away once too often and she would stop giving. Had that happened today?

He glanced down at the worn carpet and knew that changing the decor wouldn't make a difference in the way she felt about him. Unlike some of the women who had pursued him, her affections couldn't be purchased by a few trinkets and a close-up view of his medals. He had to earn his place in her life. He wasn't sure he even knew how to start. But that didn't matter either. He couldn't claim her; he had no right.

If there could be no permanent relationship between them, perhaps he could mend what they had for now. The days were slipping by, and he didn't want to think what would happen to him when she was gone.

"I'm not very good at this relationship thing," he said at last.

She didn't answer. He could feel her gaze upon him. The shadows seemed to mock his feeble attempts to apologize for what had happened earlier today. He wanted to run; this would accomplish nothing. But he held his place and shoved his hands in his pockets. He owned it to himself to try. More importantly, he owed it to her.

"I've never had to work at it before," he said, then cleared his throat. "Women always came and went. I didn't think about it because as long as they met certain requirements, I didn't care who I was with."

"Sort of like dating Barbie," she said, her voice low and husky.

He strained to see her face, but she was sitting too far back. "Exactly," he said. "Interchangeable parts."

"So I could send down my assistant and you wouldn't notice the difference?"

He smiled. "I wish that was true, Jessie, but it's not. I know it's you I'm with. I know your taste and smell and the way you feel. I listen for your voice. You are unique."

She leaned forward until her face was in the light. The lamp highlighted the dark circles under her eyes and her swollen mouth. She looked as if she'd been emotionally battered, and he cursed himself for daring to hurt her.

"That's good, because my assistant is a guy." She tried to smile, but failed miserably.

Inside his chest, in a spot near the place where his dreams had died, he felt an ache for her. He took a step closer. "Jessie, I care about you."

She looked down. Her thick hair swung forward, hiding her face. "What does that mean?"

"It means I don't want to think about your leaving."

She glanced at him. "You still don't get it, do you, Mike? I'm here because I have no choice in the matter. From the moment I saw you that first morning, you've sucked me in. I don't know how much of it is the way you look, your pain, or the courage you do your damnedest to hide. I can't figure it out. But I will. And when I know what it is about you that makes me love you, I will find a cure and get the hell away from you."

He knelt in front of her and pulled her close. She clung to him as if they'd been parted for years. "Not tonight," he whispered. "Please, Jessie, not tonight."

"Not tonight," she agreed.

* * *

It was mid-afternoon when Jessie heard the knock on the door. Because of the phone call she'd received the previous day, she'd spent the last two hours hanging around inside the house. Every time Mrs. McGregor or Grady walked by, she pretended to be on the phone with one of her suppliers, or busily working on a sketch. They didn't seem to notice anything was going on, she told herself, as she brushed her damp palms on her shorts. It was only her guilty conscience that kept seeing accusations in everyone else's eyes.

She opened the front door and stared at the young man standing on the porch. He wore gray slacks and a long-sleeved blue shirt rolled up to the elbows. His brown hair was cut painfully short, but that was probably the Navy's doing. He had freckles, and what at a stretch could be called a moustache. A good-looking kid. She knew he was nineteen now, but he looked about sixteen, and frightened enough to be picking up his first date.

"You must be Tim Evans," she said, holding out her hand to the young man.

"Yes, ma'am." He shook her hand and tried to smile. "Thank you for calling me, Mrs. Layton. I'm real grateful for the chance to come talk to Commander Coburn."

Jessie ushered him into the living room and offered him a seat. He perched on the edge of the sofa and stared expectantly at her.

"Yes, well, Commander Coburn, ah, Mike, doesn't know about your visit."

Tim look confused.

Jessie drew in a deep breath. She sat in the leather chair opposite the couch, then sprang back to her feet and started pacing the room.

Two days ago, when Mike had lashed out at her in the barn and tossed her love back in her face, she'd fled to the house to try and figure out what she should do. In a fit of determination to exorcise him from her heart, she'd found the envelope from Tim's mother's letter. Calling information for the small farm town, she'd gotten the number, then phoned Tim himself. They agreed he would stop by the ranch on his way back to his ship. Yesterday he called with his approximate arrival time. Since then, she'd vacillated between knowing she was doing the right thing and wondering if there was still time to stop Tim's visit. In the end, she'd let her plan go forward. She had to, for Mike's sake.

"The Commander doesn't want to see me, does he?" Tim asked.

"No." Jessie stopped pacing and smiled at the young man. At his age he shouldn't have to worry about someone else's problems. He should be thinking about girls and careers and going to a party on Friday night.

"I thought he might change his mind." Tim rose to his feet. "I understand that he didn't." He swallowed hard. His Adam's apple rose and lowered in his scrawny throat. "After what he said to me at the hos-pital." His voice cracked. He blinked. "I just wanted to tell him that I'm real sorry."

Jessie's heart went out to the boy. She took his arm and settled him back on the couch. He sat with his elbows on his knees.

"If you could have seen him on the carrier, ma'am," Tim said earnestly, turning his head to look at her. Tears filled his hazel eyes.

"Call me Jessie," she said and put her arm around him.

"He was a fine officer. He always took time to talk to his men. Everyone respected him." Tim roughly brushed his forearm across his eyes. "I wanted to be just like him. And it's my fault that he can't fly again."

The tears flowed in earnest. Jessie shifted until she was facing him, then pulled him into her arms. His thin body shook with the power of his sobs. Her heart ached.

"He told me he wanted me dead," Tim said, his voice muffled against her shoulder. "I'd do it too, if I could. If it would make a difference. The Commander deserves to be flying. What am I good for anyway? Anyone can work a farm. It takes someone special to be a pilot."

"Don't say that." Jessie grabbed his shoulders and tried to shake him. Skinny as he was, the young man topped her by about eight inches and out-weighed her by thirty pounds. "Don't you dare say that. Your life is as precious as Mike's. As anyone's. You don't have the right to give that away. Do you hear me?"

His hazel eyes met her. His face was pale and his freckles stood out like painted dots. He had his whole life in front of him, she thought, wishing fate had been more kind.

Looking at him made her feel a hundred years old. For him the world was still a black and white place. She'd learned about all the shades of gray. It was a hard lesson, and one that Tim would have to learn on his own.

"It's not your fault," she said softly.

She saw his mouth twist in disbelief. "No offense, ma'am—"

"Jessie."

He nodded. "Jessie. No offense, but you weren't there. If I'd been paying attention, I would never have walked behind that jet. If Mike hadn't had to pull me clear, he'd be fine now. He'd be in the Navy where he belongs, flying jets."

Tim's words were like a knife wound to her belly. If Mike was still in the Navy, he wouldn't be here with her. He wouldn't be loving her each night, making her feel special and wanted. He would still be with Pam. But Tim didn't need to hear all that. He'd come here to make his peace, and she was going to do everything in her power to see that he got his chance.

She released the boy and leaned back against the sofa. "You made a mistake," she said. "You ever do that before?"

For the first time, she saw him smile. It made him look even younger. "Yes, ma'am, ah, Jessie. Lots a times. When I was little, I'd forget to feed the pigs and my ma would come after me with a switch."

"This was just a mistake, Tim. Nothing else. Mike happened to be there. He happened to save you. Yes, you should be grateful to him, but you have no control over what went on after that. Ruining you life because you feel guilty takes away from Mike's sacrifice. You are wasting Mike's gift to you."

He looked confused. His brows drew together. "He didn't give me a gift."

"What would you call having the opportunity to live out your life?"

"I—" He glanced at his hands. "I don't know."

"Mike acted instinctively, Tim. He would have done it for anyone. As much as he beats himself up for being a bastard, he has a good heart. Now you're going to go talk to him. He won't want to listen, but you have to make him. He's going to say some pretty bad things."

"Nothing I haven't already told myself."

"Maybe not, but whatever he says, you make sure you say your piece, too. You aren't going to make him better. He's never going to be happy that he can't fly. But if you can let this go and get on with you life, then you've given Mike the next best thing. You've made his sacrifice worthwhile."

He looked at her. The tears were gone, and he didn't seem quite as haunted. "Thank you for telling me this."

"You're welcome." She leaned over and kissed his cheek, then scrambled to her feet. "Just remember, you're not going to be able to change him. You can't fix anyone. Lord knows, I've tried it enough."

"Thank you, Jessie."

Tim rose and followed her through the kitchen. Mrs. McGregor was baking cookies. She glanced curiously at the young man, but didn't ask any questions.

"He's in the barn," Jessie said. "Grooming the horses. Like I said, he'll probably try to bite your head off. Stand your ground, Tim. Despite everything, you didn't do anything worse than make a mistake. Tell him you're going to use his gift of life for as long as you have it."

The young man nodded and pushed open the back door. When it banged shut behind him, Jessie leaned against the frame and sighed. Please Lord, let her be doing the right thing.

"Is that who I think it is?" Mrs. McGregor asked from behind her.

"Yes. Tim Evans. The boy who caused Mike's accident."

"Does Mike know he's here?"

"No."

Mrs. McGregor surprised her by coming up and placing her hand on her shoulder. "I sure hope that man knows what he's got in you, Jessie. I hope he's smart enough to hold on tight and never let you go."

"Me, too."

She gave the older woman a smile and retreated to the bedroom she now shared with Mike. As she lay on the bedspread, she thought about Tim and what she'd told him. She hoped he understood that he couldn't fix Mike, that all he could do was say what he'd come for and hope for the best.

She closed her eyes and remembered Brandon. How long had she tried to change and fix him? All their married life. She'd never gotten anywhere. She wasn't faring any better with Mike. Looks like she was doomed to failure in the fix-it department.

She rolled onto her stomach and stared out the window. From the second story window, she could see the roof of the barn, but little else. She didn't know what was happening there.

She hoped Tim took her words to heart. If he could realize he was only responsible for his own life and no one else's then . . .

Jessie blinked. She slid over the side of the bed and sat up. Tim was only responsible for his life. It wasn't his fault Mike got hurt. It was an accident. It wasn't her fault either. She bit her lower lip. Her thoughts were a little fuzzy, but they were getting clearer.

It wasn't her fault that Mike was injured. He wasn't her responsibility. She didn't *have* to fix him. It wasn't even her job. She could love him and be there for him, but she didn't have to make it right.

She drew in a deep breath. Brandon. Was it the same with him? Had he *not* been her responsibility? Had it been his life to control? She remembered how she asked him to take time off, to rest, to be with her, but he'd always said no. She had tried, but he had refused her help. She had loved him, but her love hadn't been enough.

No, she thought firmly. Her love had been enough. More than enough. He had *chosen* not to change. He'd *chosen* not to be there for her. It was nothing to do with her and everything to do with him.

It was the same with Mike. She could give him everything she had, but the choice to heal or not, to admit he was whole or not, was entirely his. She grinned. It was as if the responsibility for everyone she'd ever care about had suddenly been lifted from her shoulders.

She rose and walked to the window. As she fingered the tan drapes, she sent up a prayer that Mike would find the courage to listen to Tim, and risk healing. She could love him, but she couldn't force him to accept that love.

Mike *had* to come around, she told herself firmly. Then she added a prayer that she wasn't fooling herself.

Mike stood in the driveway and watched the rental car drive away. He felt as if he'd run fifteen miles. Sweat coated his back and his hands trembled. But it was done.

A soft scuffing sound caught his attention. He turned and saw Jessie standing on the porch. He walked over to her. She came to meet him. Her brown eyes held equal parts of guilt, hope and love. At least he told himself it was love. He wished he had the faith, or courage, or whatever it took to believe her completely. Not that believing would change anything. The measure of a man is made by what he does. He looked up at the sky. He wasn't going to be any more than he was right now.

"You called him," he said, not asking a question.

She stepped down from the porch. "Yes."

Mike drew in a deep breath. "He's some farm kid from Nebraska."

"Iowa," she said, still holding onto the stair's railing. She bit her lower lip.

"Same thing. He's a fourth generation farmer." Mike shook his head. "He should never have been allowed out on that ship."

"Maybe he wanted to see the world." The hope in her eyes got brighter. He knew she was waiting for him to explode, but that wasn't going to happen.

"He made me feel old," Mike admitted, moving closer to her.

"Me, too."

He touched her cheek and smiled. "I'm still sorry I can't fly, but I'm not sorry he's alive."

"Oh, Mike."

Jessie flung herself at him. She raised her mouth to his and kissed him as if he'd single-handedly conquered the world.

"I knew you would change your mind if you could just talk to him," she murmured between kisses.

"Don't be so quick to think I've changed," he said, taking her by the arms and setting her away from him. "I'm not sure what I'd do if I ever got that second chance."

"I know," she said confidently. "Because I know the kind of man you are. I love you."

The first time her words had caught him off guard. This time he was prepared for them, but that didn't mean they hurt any less. "Sweet Jessie." He bent down and kissed her forehead. Then he touched her thick hair and inhaled her spicy perfume. "Don't love me."

Her gaze narrowed. "What now? You're secretly a woman?"

In spite of the pain, he smiled. "Worse. I can't marry you."

Although her expression didn't change, he felt her body flinch. "I don't recall asking," she said casually, as if it were of no importance.

"All women want to get married."

"I'm not all women."

She stepped away from him. A week ago he would have tried to hold her in place. Today, he let her have all the space she needed, no matter how much it hurt to let her go.

"I care about you," he said. "More than I've ever cared about any woman."

"Then tell me you love me. Just say the words."

"I can't. I have nothing to offer." He looked down at his hand.

"Is this about money?" she asked, sounding outraged.

"Not exactly. But I want to be able to give my wife something. I want to be able to provide for her."

She waved her arm toward the lodge. "What about the ranch? What about the horses and the rodeo and the guests due to arrive in a few days. Are you planning to starve out here? Are you opening this business as a charity?"

"Compared to Ross Construction, it must seem that way to you."

"This is all about male pride, isn't it?"

He shrugged. "In a way. I won't offer you less than you already have."

She began to tremble. She folded her arms over her chest and shook her head. "Oh, Mike, if only you could see I don't have anything of value. I can't hold a share of stock and let it warm me. My corporate car doesn't care how I feel. It was never about money or power. Not with Brandon, and not with you, either. I only ever wanted you to love me."

He was destroying her. He could see it in the way she seemed to fold in on herself. The life left her eyes and her mouth quivered with suppressed emotion.

"Loving you isn't enough, Jessie. Because I'm not enough."

"Isn't that my decision?" she asked desperately, openly pleading now. "Can't I be the one to say what I need? It's my life. If I chose to spend it with you, then let me."

"I can't," he said, and turned away. "Don't you know how much I wish I could? But how am I supposed to spend the rest of my life as your husband, knowing you settled for second best?"

Fifteen

He was grooming one of the horses when Jessie entered the barn. At the sight of her, his heart rate increased. With the setting sun behind her, and a bright sleeveless dress whispering around her

calves, she looked like an ancient goddess come to find a mortal
mate. She was, he knew, Mother Earth, and all things new. She grew
plants, plied her magic with color and paint and furniture, and gave
her entire being in the process of loving someone. Letting her go
would be the hardest thing he'd ever had to do. He suspected in a
couple of years he would begin to figure out it was harder than not
being able to fly. But he wouldn't ask her to stay when he had nothing
to offer.

He expected her to tell him that it was time for dinner. Instead
she handed him a piece of paper. It was a name and phone number.

"What is this?" he asked, staring at the sheet.

"The answer to your prayers," she said, her voice oddly thick, as
if she was fighting back tears.

"Jessie?"

"Call them," she said, pointing to the phone in the stable. "Call
them and get your heart's desire. And when you have it back, remember that I loved you."

Before he could ask her what she meant, she turned and hurried
out of the barn.

Mike frowned, then walked over to the plain black phone and
dialed the number. He identified himself and asked to speak to the
person Jessie said had called. When the man came on the line, Mike
leaned against the wall and prepared to listen.

"You're a hard man to track down, Commander Coburn," Sam
Vernon said.

"I'm not in the Navy any more, Mr. Vernon."

"So I've heard. I also heard about your accident. How's the
hand?"

Mike flexed it. "Better."

"Good enough to fly?"

Jessie was in the kitchen when she heard his *whoop* of excitement.
Grady looked up from his dinner and grinned.

"Guess that means our boy said yes."

"Guess it does," Jessie said, hoping she didn't sound as sad as
she felt.

Mike burst through the door. He looked around until he saw her,
then came over and gathered her into his arms. "They want me to

fly for them." He spun her around her room. His face was alive with excitement, his eyes burning with a fire she'd only seen when they made love. He grin threatened to split his face in two. "Jets. They want me to fly jets."

Mike bumped into Mrs. McGregor who gave him an indulgent smile before slapping his arm. "You'll make that poor girl sick to her stomach. Now set her down and wash up for supper. Your news can wait until then."

Mike slowly let Jessie slide to the ground. He bent over and kissed her, then winked at Mrs. McGregor. After slapping Grady on the back, he moved to the sink and started washing his hands.

"It's a private company," he said. "They've been contracted by the Navy to teach flying. They want me to come down for an interview next week. If it goes well, I'll be an instructor for them. First on the ground, while I work with a physical therapist, then up in the air." He wiped his hands dry and stared out the window. "Jets, they told me. Then possibly some experimental aircraft."

Jessie took her place at the table. He'd finally gotten the one thing he wanted. He would return to his precious skies. All thoughts of mortal things, such as the ranch, would be left behind. Her heart felt as if it was being ripped in two. A part of her loved him enough to be genuinely pleased that he finally had a chance at happiness. But the rest of her cried out at being as disposable and easily forgotten as the ranch.

Mrs. McGregor served dinner, then left for home. Mike went on about the job offer. They were mailing him more information, along with application forms.

"I'd have to live in San Diego," he said, then reached for another roll.

"I figured that," Grady said. "I can replace you. It won't be easy, but don't you give the ranch another thought."

Mike flashed him a grateful smile. "Thanks. I knew you'd understand."

Jessie wished she could understand. He'd worked so hard at the ranch. In the last few weeks he'd really seemed to grow to like it. How could he just walk away? What about the plans for the rodeo arena? What about the mare that was about to foal? What about . . . She swallowed hard. *What about me?*

Mike and Grady talked excitedly for the rest of the meal. Jessie pushed her food around on her plate and told herself that she would get over Mike. She'd been destroyed when Brandon had died, and she'd been able to get on with her life.

But it's not the same, she thought, fighting a wave of sadness. Brandon had died. There hadn't been any second chance with him. But Mike was leaving her because he wanted to. That made it worse. Because it could have worked if only Mike would have let it. Besides, she'd never loved Brandon as much as she loved Mike. She'd cared about her husband, but he hadn't been her soul mate.

"If you'll excuse me," Grady said, rising from the table. "I want to check on our pregnant mare, then I'm going to turn in." He hold out his hand. "I'm proud of you, Mike."

Mike shook hands with him. Jessie remembered the first morning she'd arrived when he wouldn't shake hands or do anything other than hide from the world. Now he was ready to conquer it again.

"You're very quiet," he said, when Grady had left.

"It's a lot to take in." She forced herself to look up at him and smile. He was so damn good-looking, she thought as her heart shattered into tiny pieces. Strong and brave. A warrior. No longer broken. It was time to send him on his way. There were battles to be fought up in the sky. Enemies to be conquered, maidens to be won. "I'm very happy for you."

"I'm glad." He grinned and leaned across the table to take her hands in his. "I can't believe I'm going to get another chance."

"It's wonderful," she agreed.

"So do you want to wait and have a big wedding, or do you want something smaller that we can arrange more quickly?"

She stared at him. "What did you say?"

"At a loss for words, Jessie? That's not like you." He cocked his head and stared at her. "Will you marry me, Jessica Layton Ross?"

"I thought you *couldn't* marry me," she blurted out.

He grinned. "That was before."

"But nothing's changed."

"Everything has changed."

Because he was a jet jockey again. Because he could sit in some million dollar piece of metal and fly faster than the speed of sound, suddenly he was whole and all she needed.

She looked across the table at Mike. He glowed with happiness. His blue eyes danced with excitement and there was an air of confidence and pride about him. He was handsome enough to take her breath away; he could love her into a passioned frenzy and tenderly hold her as she slept. He could claim her, heart and soul, but until this minute, she had not known him.

All that Grady had told her suddenly made sense. She'd thought she understood what it had meant to Mike to be a fighter pilot, but she'd been wrong about everything. Except for the fact that she loved him.

She squeezed his hands tightly, then released him. "I can't marry you, Mike."

He grinned. "Go ahead, make me squirm. I deserve it."

"I'm not kidding."

His smile faded. "Jessie, I thought you . . . cared about me."

He couldn't even say the word "love," she thought sadly. It was so far removed from his world. "I love you, Mike, but I won't marry a fighter pilot."

He folded his arms on the table. "If it's about other women, I promise I'll be completely faithful. You've got to believe that. I never bothered before, because I didn't care. But Jessie, you're the best thing that's ever happened to me."

"No," she said slowly, wondering when the pain was going to hit. "Flying is the best thing that ever happened to you. I didn't mind coming in second to another woman, but I won't compete with your career. I've already done that, and it's too destructive. I almost lost myself with Brandon. If I were to do the same thing with you, I would never survive."

"Wait a minute." He rose to his feet and glared down at her. He raised his right hand and stuck out his thumb. "First, there is no other woman. You're not coming in second. If you're referring to Pam, she could parade around this ranch naked for weeks, and I'd never be tempted. Second," he raised his index finger, "there's no competition with my career. It's practically a nine-to-five job. I won't be going to sea on long cruises. It's completely safe. Think of it as a desk job with wings." He smiled winningly. "And third, I can't do this thing without you, Jessie. I need you."

But he wouldn't say that he loved her. "I'm not afraid of losing you to a crash," she said, and rose to her feet. She walked around the table and touched his arm. "It's the day-to-day being shut out that frightens me. If you wanted to do anything else, be an engineer, raise cattle, work for a bank, I would support you a hundred percent. But when you fly, you are what you do. You've allowed your career to define your life. That is your choice, but it's not one I can live with. When you allow yourself to get pulled in that deep, you can't come out for anything. Not even a wife. I won't be shut out that way. If I get married again, I want it to be a partnership, not a part-time convenience."

"It wouldn't be like that," he said, staring down at her. "I give you my word. We would be partners."

"How?" She shook her head sadly. "I wish I could explain it better, Mike. This probably sounds selfish and melodramatic to you, but the truth is, I was a widow long before Brandon died. I can't go through that again." She stared at the floor and then looked back at him. She could see she was tearing him apart, but it wasn't enough. He still didn't get it. "Here we have something together. On this ranch, our lives mesh."

He drew his brows together. "On this ranch, I'm nothing."

"On this ranch, you are everything, because you are yourself. You define who you are by what's inside, not what you do. I love this ranch. I want to remodel the house and have children here with you. I would give it up, if that's what you wanted. I would move anywhere in the world for you. But I won't marry a fighter pilot. I won't become one of the walking wounded again."

His blue eyes grew hard. "Don't make me choose, Jessie."

"You've already made your choice." She took a deep breath and let it out slowly. "I never had a chance."

The day Mike left for his interview, Jessie finished decorating the ranch. She stood in the center of one of the private cottages and stared at the pretty room. There was a living area on one side, then the bedroom. She'd chosen rose and blue as the color scheme. The carpet was plush under her feet, the furnishings elegant. She walked into the spacious bathroom and adjusted the towels on the rack. Everything was done; she had no reason to stay.

The trailer was packed up and would be taken back to the company warehouse that afternoon. Her clothes and personal belongings were still in Mike's room, but she could be ready to go in less than an hour. She'd already called to have someone come down and drive the company van to San Francisco.

She should leave. It would be easier while Mike was gone. Good-byes would only make a difficult situation worse.

She walked over to the lodge. All of the construction workers had left. A couple of guys were still planting shrubs along the walk-way and stringing lights, but other than that, the ranch was quiet. Grady was working with the horses, and Mrs. McGregor was in the kitchen cooking dinner.

Jessie walked through the main room of the lodge. It had turned out exactly as she had pictured it. Light flooded the area from the huge windows. Rugs and furniture were scattered around creating conversation areas. The twelve foot registration desk angled across one corner.

She inhaled the smell of fresh cut wood, paint and new furniture. She'd saved the antiques for the bedrooms and had used strong durable pieces in the public rooms. If she closed her eyes, she could imagine this placed filled with guests. Families, young couples on a romantic getaway, retired seniors coming to commune with nature. If she concentrated, she could see her and Mike here, growing old together, raising a family. It could have been perfect.

She opened her eyes and smiled. Okay, with the way she and Mike often fought, maybe perfect wasn't the right word. But it would have been a wonderful marriage full of passion and caring and love.

She continued across the hardwood floor and started down the hall. One closed door called to her. Since her first day, she hadn't been in there. Now, as her way of saying good-bye, she turned the knob and pushed open the door.

Dress whites still hung by the door. Boxes stacked together and model planes covered a table against the wall. She could see the piles of photographs and the framed medals. His helmet was where she'd left it. She picked it up and traced the letters on the back. *Rogue Warrior.*

"I thought I'd find you here."

She looked up and saw Grady standing in the doorway. "I'm just having a last look," she said, and set the helmet down.

"So you'll be leaving us." His bushy eyebrows pulled together.

"I don't see any other way."

"I'm sorry to hear that, little lady. I'd gotten used to having you around."

She blinked hard to fight the tears. "I'd gotten used to being around. But with Mike going to work in San Diego . . ."

"Is your job so important to you that you won't consider moving?"

She touched the framed medals. Her finger outlined their shape on the cool glass. "No, I've been doing the decorating because I really enjoy it and I needed something to fill the time. I would have given it up to be here with Mike."

"But you won't give it up to watch him fly jets." He wasn't asking a question.

She looked at the older man. He leaned against the door frame and folded his arms over his chest. "Am I wrong, Grady?"

"You're the only one who can answer that."

"I know. I keep telling myself it shouldn't matter what Mike does for a living. I wouldn't care if he drove a bus or collected garbage or just wanted to make a go of the ranch. But the flying. I can't stand by and watch him do that."

"Are you afraid he'll crash and die?"

"No." She walked over to the uniform. After pulling up the dry cleaner bag, she touched the heavy fabric and smoothed the sleeves. "I loved my husband, Brandon. But that didn't matter to him. His first love was his work. Mike's first love is flying. Maybe I'm selfish, but I'm tired of being second best in someone's life."

"Mike loves you."

She stared at the row of buttons, then touched each one. "I'd like to believe you, but he can't even say the words."

"That doesn't mean he's not thinking them, or feeling them in his heart."

"I doesn't do me much good if he keeps his feelings bottled up inside."

"Men don't always say a lot. They show their feelings by what they do."

She bit her lower lip and drew the plastic covering back in place. "Then why did Mike leave me, Grady? Isn't that showing that he doesn't love me?"

"You've got it turned around. He's taking the job because he cares. It's his way of making things right between you."

His way of being enough, she thought sadly. "Why can't he see he's fine the way he is? Why does he have to go back to those damn jets?"

She felt Grady walk up behind her. He put his hands on her shoulders and squeezed her gently. "Maybe it's not Mike you're afraid of. Maybe it's you."

She turned and faced him. "Maybe I'm frightened of committing and then losing again?" she asked.

He nodded. His blue eyes looked so wise. She wished she could risk believing him about all of it.

"I've thought of that," she admitted. "I've wondered if I'm trying to stack the deck in my favor. I know that, I don't want to lose Mike to a job, but I also know that his returning to flying is really pushing my buttons. I'm so confused, Grady. I don't know what to do."

He gave her a smile. "When we were at sea and there was a storm we couldn't outrun, we used to turn the ship into the wind. Meet it head on. It's the safest way. Go through quickly and get it over with."

"I'm afraid."

"You love that boy, and he loves you."

"What if I'm not enough? What if I don't have the strength to do this?"

"If you don't try, you've lost him anyway."

She flung herself at Grady and let the older man's embrace comfort her. "I can't lose him. I love him too much."

"Then I'd say you'll find the strength."

Mike parked close to the runway and got out of the Porche. He could see the gleaming jet, poised like a bird of prey, waiting for an unseen command to hurl it high into the heavens.

The grumbling roar of the engines grew to a high-pitched scream. The beautiful machine rolled down the runway, picking up speed until it broke free of the confines of gravity and soared away toward the sun.

Mike leaned against his car and stared until the jet was out of sight. He waited almost half an hour until there was another plane ready for take-off, then he watched that one fly away as well. He spent the better part of the morning by the runway, seeing jet after jet take off. He watched them land, and the pilots emerge. He didn't bother to go over and greet any of them even though there were better than even odds he would know a couple of the guys. The fence between the road and the runway reminded him that he wasn't a part of that world anymore. He was on the other side.

He got in his car and drove toward the terminal building. His visitor's pass got him inside. Here the noise from the jet's engines vibrated everything. He inhaled the familiar smells, recognized uniforms and rankings. But no one saluted. He wasn't an officer anymore. He had returned to a place that had been as much a part of his life as breathing, and yet he was a stranger. It wasn't just his hand that made him different.

He paused by a bank of phones and thought about calling the ranch. For the last four days he'd battled the need to hear Jessie's voice. Through a series of interviews and medical evaluations. Through a simulated flight that had been almost as good as the real thing. He'd come to San Diego to find a job and a way to be whole again. He'd found everything he'd been missing in his life. Was the price of that losing Jessie?

He picked up a receiver and punched in the phone number and his calling card number. After two rings, Grady picked up the phone.

"It's Mike."

"I figured you'd be calling," the old man said.

"How's the pregnant mare?"

"If you're going to be moving to San Diego, you'd better get used to not being in charge. Or didn't they offer you the job?"

"Answer my question, old man," Mike said, grinning. "Then I'll answer yours."

"The mare's fine. The vet thinks she's going to foal this weekend."

"They made me the offer."

"Hot damn. I knew you could do it, son." He could hear Grady's pride and pleasure at his accomplishment.

"Thanks. I sweated out a simulation, but I hadn't forgotten a thing. My range of motion is really coming back. I saw a doctor. He's suggested minor surgery to do some fine-tuning, but other than that, I'm on the road to recovery."

Mike asked a couple more questions about the upcoming opening. He didn't bother listening to the answers. He was waiting for his friend to mention Jessie. Finally Mike gripped the receiver. "You're not going to tell me if she's still there, are you?"

"You asking?"

He thought about Jessie telling him that even without being a pilot he was enough for her. That all she wanted from him was his love. He remembered how relieved he'd been by the job offer. Secure in the knowledge that he could once again fly jets, he could now go back and claim her.

"I'm not asking," he said quietly.

"Then I'm not saying."

But if she'd left him, Grady would have said. His friend wouldn't have let him hope if everything was lost. She was waiting for him. He could have it all.

Mike didn't remember telling Grady good-bye or hanging up the phone. He didn't remember walking through the terminal and out onto the runway. It wasn't until his hand touched the cool skin of an F-14 that he realized where he was.

"Hi, baby," he murmured as he stroked the jet. He'd landed beauties like this one on carriers in the dead of night, during storms, and in perfect weather. He'd spent about three years of his life at sea. He'd been round the world, he'd watched friends die.

Deliberately, he touched the side of the plane with his scarred hand as if the energy of the jet could magically heal him. He stared, but the scars remained in place.

If Jessie waited for him at the ranch, she'd changed her mind. She would risk him flying jets, she would risk being second best in his life. He bowed his head, humbled by the depth of her love.

"Excuse me, sir, should you be here?" a serviceman in a mechanic's uniform asked as he approached.

Mike showed him his visitor's pass.

"I'm sorry, sir," the kid said, "but you're not cleared for this area."

"I know," Mike said. "I was just leaving."

Jessie sketched in the last few lines, then leaned back in the kitchen chair and stretched. As she'd wanted to since she'd first seen Mike's house, she'd finally done the drawings to remodel the interior. The downstairs only needed minor modifications. She'd added an enclosed sun room on the side of the house, and a big porch out front. The garden needed redoing, she thought as she penciled in a row of climbing roses. There was plenty of room on the side for a swing set. She smiled. That was for later.

The upstairs had taken her the most time. She combined three of the six bedrooms to make a large master suite with a huge bathroom, walk-in closet and Jacuzzi tub. She'd put a fireplace in the corner of the sitting area, and drawn in country French furniture. She smiled at the sketch and wondered if Mike would like it.

The back door opened.

"About time, Grady," she said, without turning around. "Your lunch is getting cold. Mrs. McGregor isn't back from the store, so I heated some soup. It's on the stove." She held up the sketch pad. "What do you think?"

"I think I love you," Mike said.

Jessie sprang to her feet and spun to face him. He stood in the doorway looking at her. He was tanned and handsome and staring at her with the most wonderful loving expression in his eyes.

"You're back," she said, and flung herself at him.

He drew her close and hugged her. "I'm back," he repeated, then bent down and kissed her.

His lips were firm and familiar. She wanted to be in his arms forever. His hands moved up and down her spine, igniting sparks of desire.

He raised his head and started to speak. Before he could say a word, she touched her finger to his mouth.

"Me first, okay?" she asked.

He nodded.

She drew in a breath. "I will move with you to San Diego, because you want to fly jets. I'll never understand it, but I love you, too much to let my fear stand in the way. I want to remodel this house and come back here on vacations though. I'd like our children to spend their summers here." She caught her breath and waited anxiously, hoping he would be happy with her decision. His slow smile threatened to melt her bones. He looked as pleased and touched as if she'd just handed him the most precious gift he could imagine.

He cupped her face in his hand. Blue eyes met and held her own. "Tell me you love me."

"I love you."

"No matter what?" He looked so serious.

"No matter what," she said.

He took her hands in his and kissed her knuckles. "I turned them down."

She stared, positive she'd heard him wrong. "You what? But I thought that's what you wanted."

He shrugged. "Flying an F-14 isn't going to fix my hand. You were right. I am who I am, and my job doesn't define that. I'm staying here, at the ranch. I want to breed horses and start a rodeo. I want to marry you and watch our children grow up here." He swallowed. "Stay here with me, Jessie. Marry me. All I have to give you is the promise that I'll love you forever. You'll always be first in my life, because you are the best part of me."

She felt the tears on her cheeks, but didn't care. "Yes, " she said and kissed him. "Yes, oh, yes." She wrapped her arms around him. "You're all I need. You've always been all I need. You're the best part of me, too."

As they clung to each other, they didn't notice that the back door opened, or see Grady smiling at them. When Mike picked her up and carried her up the stairs and into their bedroom, they didn't hear the older man humming to himself as he ate his lunch.

Jessie watched Mike's face as he carefully undressed her. When they were both naked, he touched her body reverently. Even as he prepared to enter her, she could see the love shining through his passion. She reached for him and held him close. The rogue warrior had found his home at last.